BBC

DOCTOR WHO

BBC

DOCTOR WHO

THE SECRET IN VAULT 13

DAVID SOLOMONS

RANDOM HOUSE 🏠 NEW YORK

Jacket illustrations by Laura Ellen Anderson
Interior illustrations by George Ermos

All rights reserved. Published in the United States by Random House Children's Books, a division of Penguin Random House LLC, New York. Originally published by Puffin Books, a division of Penguin Random House Ltd., London, in 2018.

Random House and the colophon are registered trademarks of Penguin Random House LLC.

Visit us on the Web! rhcbooks.com

Educators and librarians, for a variety of teaching tools, visit us at RHTeachersLibrarians.com

Library of Congress Cataloging-in-Publication Data is available upon request.
ISBN 978-1-9848-9598-1 (hardcover) — ISBN 978-1-9848-9600-1 (lib. bdg.) — ISBN 978-1-9848-9599-8 (ebook)

Printed in the United States of America

10 9 8 7 6 5 4 3 2 1

First Edition

For Natasha, Luke and Lara.

Contents

1. Diddly-dum
Diddly-dum Woo-woo

It was a Mark VI combat mechanical and it had been hunting them since daybreak. The machine had pursued them through the Forest of Desolation, across the Burning Grounds, into the Valley of Agonies, and to this place. Now the chase was all but over.

The Mark VI adjusted its stealth settings and edged closer to the cave. Inside, the four humans had chosen to make their last stand. During the long pursuit, the machine had assessed each of their capabilities, finding none to be a match for its own.

1

It ran through their profiles now.

First, the younger male human, designation Ryan. Minimal offensive capabilities. Unarmoured. Unlike the Mark VI's active phlebotinum armour, his cellulose-based clothing provided no effective protection. Similarly, although his rubber-and-plastic shoes offered traction, they were no match for its military-grade tank tracks.

The machine accessed the next profile: the younger female human, designation Yaz. Her actions during the pursuit had demonstrated evidence of military or law-enforcement training, however it was clear that she lacked battle experience. The Mark VI, meanwhile, had seen action across the known galaxy in the service of the Fleet before it had been drafted to the Citadel. She posed no threat.

Next, the older male human, designation Graham. Eyesight fading, bone density weak, hairline receding. He would be crushed as easily as a bugbeast of Zeta Draconis. It took a microsecond to dismiss him.

And, finally, the other female human. The Mark VI had obtained little intelligence about her during the pursuit besides the fact that she was clearly the group's leader.

Before launching the assault that would inevitably lead to their capture, the Mark VI took a moment to scan the humans one final time. Its finely tuned audio-detection circuits picked up a snatch of conversation.

'I wouldn't call it a *giant* robot,' said the female leader. 'Don't exaggerate, Graham.'

'Well, excuse me, Doc. I didn't know there was a minimum height requirement.'

The Mark VI analysed Graham's voice. The waveform suggested anxiety, along with the characteristic known as sarcasm.

'All I know,' he went on, 'is that we're being chased by a bloomin' great metal monster.'

'Actually, it's not metal,' said the woman the Mark VI now knew to be designated Doc. 'The shell is some kind of composite material. Ray-shielded, but not invulnerable. Anyway, I've seen everything I need to. That's enough running around for one day.'

'What are you talking about?' said Graham.

'You planned this, didn't you?' said Ryan. 'I knew it!'

'You mean I didn't have to knacker myself running all over this planet?' Graham protested.

'How else was I supposed to figure out what we were up against?' said Doc. 'Had to give our friend a proper run-out.'

The Mark VI paused. Its audio scan had detected something unexpected.

3

Ba-doom. Ba-doom.

Overlapping heartbeats, emanating from Doc. The machine drew the only logical conclusion: she had two hearts. It made the necessary correction to the profiles. Three humans. One unknown.

Identify.

The Mark VI connected to the Fleet network, and sent its query winging back to the Citadel's supercomputers, accessing the knowledge of 10,000 star systems. Four milliseconds later, it had an answer.

Species: Time Lord.

Origin: Gallifrey.

Designation: The Doctor.

A list of the most dangerous species in the universe scrolled across the Mark VI's display: Sontarans, Cybermen, the Daleks of Skaro. According to the database, they had all fallen to this Doctor's sword. Not that the machine could actually identify a sword – or indeed any kind of weapon at all – on her person.

The Mark VI hesitated.

Until that moment, every factor had pointed to an overwhelming victory in its favour, but this new information prompted it to inject a note of caution into its plan. Rather than risk close combat with a being so obviously lethal, the machine adjusted its tactics, choosing instead to launch a ranged attack. Selecting its primary armament – a plasma-beam blaster built into its right arm – the Mark VI activated the laser rangefinder and calculated a firing solution.

'No good,' said Yaz, returning from the back of the cave. 'It's a dead end.' She pointed to the cave's mouth. 'That's our only way out.'

'Are you sure that robot thing's even still out there?' asked Ryan, squinting into the fast-fading daylight. 'Maybe we gave it the slip.'

With a noise like a great gulp, the interior of the cave suddenly bloomed the colour of storm-light. The air sizzled and a burning smell filled the small space, as Ryan scrambled frantically towards the back of the cave. Looking over his shoulder, he saw the boulder he had been sheltering behind was split cleanly down the middle, as neatly sliced as a loaf of bread.

'And I suppose that isn't a death ray,' grumbled Graham, brushing stone fragments out of his hair.

'Oh, that's definitely a death ray.' The Doctor grinned.

Ryan and Yaz shared a look.

'I've seen that grin before,' Ryan whispered. 'On Proxima Ceti, just before she outwitted those carnivorous chessmen.'

Yaz nodded. 'And on that derelict space station, when she worked out how to defuse the temporal anomaly bomb with three seconds left on the countdown.'

'Couldn't have done it without you,' the Doctor said, striding past them.

Ryan hadn't travelled with the Doctor for long, but even in their short time together he had seen her make impossible escapes more times than Harry Houdini – and one time he'd even seen her escape from Houdini. Well, not the real Houdini, but 200 evil cyborg clones of the great escapologist in the subways of New York City in 1904. But that was another story. What, he wondered as he watched her march towards the cave entrance, could she possibly have planned now?

The Doctor stopped beneath the stone arch at the cave's mouth. This planet had a short day–night cycle, and the sun was already low on the horizon. The last of its slanting rays cast a golden aura around the Doctor's silhouette. Standing there, glowing, she looked invincible – perhaps even immortal.

She raised both hands.

'We surrender!' she called out.

The Citadel rose twelve kilometres out of the Blasted Plains, a shining tower of iridanium steel. It was protected from every kind of weapon in the known galaxies – atomic, plasma, psionic and more – and from the endless buffeting of the tropospheric winds by force-field technology developed in its labs.

The builders and occupiers of this tower were the Fleet, a space-faring humanoid race who, having devastated their own world in a series of wars, were hungry to acquire new ones. The first ninety-seven levels of the Citadel were administrative offices. No one considered paperwork before embarking on a galactic war – no one, that is, except the Fleet. Above Admin lay Research and Development (levels ninety-eight through 112), Communications, Planning, Medical and, finally, at the pinnacle, the Space Lord himself.

From his throne room in the sky, the Space Lord waited for the strangers. News of their capture had come in over the network barely half a cycle earlier, and they would be brought into his presence shortly. Curious to observe their arrival, he watched through the great curved window set high above the Blasted Plains, despite the fact that he knew he was too high up to spot them at the Citadel doors, even with the famed eyesight of his kind.

7

From his spot here in the highest room in the tower, he could see more if he looked up than if he gazed down. Raising his head, he saw the flash of laser-welding equipment from the busy shipyards in low-orbit. The construction of three new dreadnoughts was nearing completion, and one of them would serve as his personal flagship in the upcoming attack on the dozing inhabitants of the mineral-rich Avolantis System.

Turning away from the window, he returned to his throne and surveyed the room in preparation for his audience. From the polished coal-black floor covering the area of two carrier decks to the triple-height doors fashioned from the hull of a captured Frost Pirate warship, it was a room designed to intimidate all who entered. The throne itself was unremarkable enough, crafted from the most precious metals in the galaxy and studded with jewels – what you'd expect.

It was the twin dorsal fins flanking the throne that really made an impression. More than ten metres high, they had been stripped from a pair of now-extinct megalovore sharks that once swam in the Outland Sea (also gone – boiled away during the Ice Cap Wars).

From the doors to the dais on which the throne sat ran a strip of red carpet lined with three two-metre-high glass cylinders on either side. It was only as visitors were guided along the path to kneel before the throne that they realised the true nature of the six glass cylinders. The First Space Lord of the Admiralty allowed himself a small smile of satisfaction as he recalled the many horrified reactions he had witnessed over the years. The cylinders were more than just ornaments; they were bottle prisons, collecting jars in which he kept his vanquished enemies alive for his amusement. Souvenirs of war. The miserable prisoners were crammed in so tightly that they had barely any room to turn their heads – and, in the case of the three-headed Hydran of Polaris Alpha, no room at all.

Five of the six jars were occupied. By the end of the day the sixth would be too. The Space Lord grimaced. That woman had been a thorn in his side ever since she had showed up with her three companions in that ridiculous (but intriguing) vessel.

Casting a glance over his shoulder into the corner of the room behind him, he saw the ridiculous vessel in question. An insignificant blue box with no obvious propulsion device and no visible weaponry, it was surrounded by a team of his finest technicians. They were all stroking their chins in puzzlement. The hiss of a plasma-cutter filled the air as they made yet another attempt to penetrate the exterior. The flame of the cutter died, and its operator flipped up her mask and shook her head. Not even a scorch-mark.

It had no force field, and yet the box had resisted every attempt to gain entry. This only made the Space Lord more eager to understand its construction. The engineering specifications of its impenetrable hull would be invaluable to his navy. He intended to extract its secrets, either from the box or from its captain.

The throne-room doors swung open on silent hinges, and he turned to face her. There she stood, at the head of her squad. The Doctor.

They hardly look like special forces sent to disrupt my activities, the Space Lord thought, *but that may well be the intention.*

His enemies were numerous and clever.

The Mark VI combat mechanical that had captured the group now herded them along the processional path. Once again, the Space Lord was pleased by the reaction to his bottle-prisons. The young human male seemed particularly shaken. *How gratifying.* The Space Lord's pleasure was tempered, however, by the Doctor.

She stopped next to the Hydran's prison and tapped on the glass. 'Have you out of there in a mo,' she said, then – for no reason that the Space Lord could comprehend – she raised both thumbs.

He experienced a sensation he hadn't felt for a very long time. It was so unusual that it took him by surprise, an uncharacteristic shudder of unease that made him glad of the presence of his elite guard. Ranks of them lined the throne room. Drawn from his most feared marine commando unit, they stood to attention in their massive powered exoskeleton suits, blast-visors covering their faces, bulky multi-barrelled blasters gripped in enhanced gloved hands.

But that was all mostly for show. The new Mark VI was the real threat: a robotic soldier, fearless, tireless, faithful and invincible. Just one could defeat an entire army of space marines. The Space Lord had five thousand of them! Soon his enemies would be crushed beneath their treads.

The prisoners were lined up before him and forced to pay their respects on their knees by the butt of a blaster. The Doctor got to her feet and took a step towards the throne. There was the instant *click-clack* of many blasters being raised, but a flick of the Space Lord's finger caused his marines to lower their weapons. He shook off his earlier apprehension. What possible harm could come to him here in the Citadel, the heart of the Fleet empire and the most secure building in the galaxy? The thought that he needed protecting from her was amusing. *He* was the one who made others cower.

It was time to inform these intruders of their terrible fate. The Space Lord decided to go with his favourite speech – the one he'd given last month to the remnants of the government of Murgon III after he'd crushed their armada. The one he always gave to defeated opponents. It was a speech at once informative and gloating, calculated to torment the vanquished at their lowest ebb. He was just preparing to launch into the rather elegant opening paragraph when the Doctor spoke first.

'What are you going to do after?'

Once again, the Space Lord felt his usually supreme self-confidence waiver. 'After what?'

'After today. When all of this is finished with.' She gestured around the throne room. 'Because you need to start thinking about the future. Maybe you could retrain.' She looked at Graham. 'They're always looking for bus drivers, right?'

Graham made a face. 'I think the intergalactic destruction might be a bit of a blot on his CV.'

12

The Space Lord slammed his fist against the arm of the throne. 'ENOUGH! I am Space Lord Draal, First Admiral of the Fleet, fourth of my line. Who are you to dare address me this way?'

'I'm the Doctor, first in the Gallifrey Undertens Swimathon, thirteenth of my line.'

She raised her hand. In it was a device the size of a dagger, but it wasn't sharp like a blade. A crystal was embedded at one end. How had it slipped through the body scan? No matter. It clearly was not a weapon. If it had been, she would already be dead. The Mark VI was programmed to respond immediately and with maximum force to any mortal threat to the Space Lord.

'We had a nice walk back to the Citadel with your giant robot here.'

'Hey, you said –' Graham began.

The Doctor waggled the device. 'Gave me just enough time to reprogram him with a little update.' She gestured to the Mark VI. 'What do you say, Bernard?'

With a whine of actuators, the Mark VI lumbered forward on its tracks, sending up a fine film of dust. The whole room shook as it rolled to the foot of the throne, then extended a massive arm. Each mechanical limb contained enough firepower to vaporise a battleship, but at that moment its metal hand contained something quite different: a small blue flower. The Mark VI offered it up.

'Have. A. Nice. Day.'

'See, Bernard here has a new set of orders,' the Doctor explained. 'Should you attempt to wage one more ridiculous war, you'll discover he doesn't like that – and neither do his five thousand friends.'

The Space Lord's unease was rapidly turning into panic. 'Five thou–' But, before he could finish, the throne-room doors flew off their hinges and crashed to the floor.

Dozens of Mark VI combat mechanicals poured through the gap.

The space marines were not only the bravest but the smartest troops in the Space Lord's navy. That's why, upon seeing the advancing robot horde, they instantly dropped their blasters in surrender.

Outside the throne room's enormous curved window, hundreds more Mark VIs hovered into view, using their antigrav engines to keep an electronic eye on the proceedings inside.

'Oh, yeah,' the Doctor said. 'When I said "update", what I meant was "virus". I replicated the new instructions across every Mark VI in your armoury. And I wouldn't try reprogramming them once I've gone.' She wagged a warning finger. 'Seriously, that would get messy. Fast.'

She swung round and pointed her not-dagger at the containment tubes. There was a hum, the crystal at the end glowed orange, and a moment later the glass prisons shattered. As their cages fell away, the occupants stumbled out of the wreckage and collapsed to the floor, gasping.

'Take them to the TARDIS,' instructed the Doctor. 'And put the kettle on.'

Yaz, Ryan and Graham helped the former prisoners to their feet, hooves or tentacles, and guided them towards the blue box behind the throne.

The Doctor produced a small key from a string round her neck, then strode across to the blue box and inserted the key into the lock below the door handle. The Space Lord and his technicians could only gawp as she swung the door open. In seconds, the group had passed inside, and only the Doctor remained, standing in the doorway of her vessel.

'I know that right now this feels like a change for the worse,' she said. 'But give it three generations – four, max – and you'll thank me.'

She stepped inside, and slammed the door shut behind her.

Over the years, the Space Lord had seen the knowledge of defeat in the eyes of a hundred opponents. Now, as his head drooped and he glanced at the polished floor, he saw it in his own reflection.

A strange sound filled the throne room. It was coming from the blue box. At first it reminded him of the howl of the Devil Bird, a creature he had hunted in the forests of his home world when he was a youth. Most of all, however, it sounded like the mocking laughter of the universe. The light on top of the blue box flashed, the vessel faded in and out of existence, and then it vanished forever.

2. Bigger on the Inside

There are three universal constants: Planck's quantum of action, toast always falling butter-side down, and the reaction of anyone entering the TARDIS for the first time. Whether they were a twelve-eyed giant spider from Metebelis III or a short-sighted earthling, their response was always the same: their eyes (two or more) would boggle, they would let out a gasp, and they'd say something like, *'Kalacha nee-too webweb!'* (Metebelin for, 'Gosh, it's bigger on the inside!')

So, once the Space Lord's former prisoners had got over their predictable amazement, Yaz led them into the depths of the TARDIS to be treated for the after-effects of their confinement. Her police instinct had kicked in automatically – it was surprising how much of the training she'd received from the Hallamshire force could be applied to dealing with alien races.

Once they all had food in their bellies – or, in the case of one, her external digestive sac – Yaz took them to the temporary accommodation where they would spend the duration of the journey back to their home worlds. The TARDIS, a considerate host, had prepared each of their rooms to suit their needs: the aquatic Dalse slipped gratefully into its acid plunge-pool, the feather-light Chentan performed a series of delighted somersaults in her zero-G suite; the Zraryx couple burrowed into their cosy lava-nest; and the three-headed Hydran sank, exhausted, into a bed covered with pillows.

In each of their reactions, Yaz saw the same exhilaration she'd felt on first coming aboard the TARDIS. She'd soon realised it wasn't just the timeship that was bigger on the inside; as soon as she stepped through its doors, *she* felt bigger and bolder too.

Meanwhile, the Doctor, Graham and Ryan gathered in the console room. Just like the Time Lords who built them, every TARDIS had two hearts: the engine room with its near-magical power source, the Eye of Harmony, and the circular console room.

Around the edges stood six pillars, each as thick as an ancient tree trunk, which seemed to grow out of the floor. The walls were a pattern of nested hexagons, lucid blue. Set into one wall was the TARDIS's main door, its design echoing the police-box exterior. Incongruous against the fantastical interior, the entrance looked like an extension forced on the architects by a plodding local-council planning department. From the police-box entrance, a hexagon-starred walkway stretched inside, pointing to the console itself. With pipes slinking around its base, the circular console was like something from the brass section of an alien orchestra. The top part was divided into several distinct sections, each boasting switches and controls for governing the TARDIS's systems. In the very centre, raised above everything else, stood what appeared to be a sand-timer. And from everywhere came the same glowing light.

No chairs. That was the first thing Graham had noticed when he had walked through the doors of the police box all those months ago. Well, obviously not the *first* thing, but the lack of furniture had become sorely apparent when he went to rest his weary bones and found he couldn't.

'But you've changed their whole way of life,' he said now, leaning against one side of the console.

He was relieved to have made it out alive from the Space Lord's freaky throne room with its shark-fin decor, and the Doctor's plan had been a total success. Thanks to her, 5,000 invincible robots were policing the bad guys, and would prevent them from starting any more wars until they eventually forgot that they were ever warmongers in the first place. Nonetheless, Graham felt vaguely uneasy about the outcome.

'I thought you weren't supposed to meddle in other civilisations,' he went on. 'Isn't it a rule? Wassit called – the Prime Directive?'

'You're thinking of *Star Trek*,' said Ryan.

'Yeah,' said the Doctor, inputting co-ordinates to the navigation system. 'Meddling's kind of my thing.'

Yaz left the recovering prisoners to sleep. For the first time in years, they had a chance of happy dreams, and soon they would be reunited with families they never imagined they'd see again.

She found the Doctor in the console room, with Ryan and Graham, carrying out running repairs to the TARDIS. The timeship sure seemed to require a lot of maintenance.

The Doctor's hand shot out from beneath a recently removed panel. 'Particle file, please.'

Ryan rooted about in a toolbox, then passed her a flat bar of rectangular metal with a wooden handle. The surface of the metal shimmered, and when Yaz looked closer it appeared to be full of stars. She could see Ryan gawp at the strange device as he handed it over to the Doctor. Although Yaz had gone to school with Ryan, she barely knew him. And, until the business with the Tzim-Sha, she'd never met Graham, his granddad. There was nothing like a bit of life-and-death struggle against an otherworldly menace to bring strangers together, though, was there?

At least Ryan and Graham were human. The Doctor was another matter. Sure, she looked and sounded like a regular earthling, but she was far from being one.

'Our guests are resting,' Yaz said.

'Shouldn't take long to drop them off,' the Doctor replied, still fiddling under the bonnet. 'Even in a TARDIS as out-of-date as this one.'

Yaz frowned. 'How can a time machine be out of date?'

'Time *and* space machine,' the Doctor corrected her. 'This is an old Type Forty, and the chameleon circuit hasn't worked for a long time. The TARDIS is supposed to blend in with its surroundings, but the exterior resembles a London police box circa 1963 because it got stuck in the sixties.'

'Like Graham,' Ryan said with a grin.

'Hey,' Graham objected. 'How old do you think I am?'

As Graham and Ryan teased each other, Yaz quietly studied the Doctor. *How old indeed?* A Time Lord's lifespan, Yaz had learned, dwarfed that of a human being, but the Doctor hadn't always lived in the same body. When her body grew too old or became irreparably damaged, she had the ability to create a new one through a process called regeneration. The Doctor was apparently on her thirteenth body.

As incredible as that was, there was something else too. The Doctor's twelve previous bodies had all been male. Yaz's mind boggled every time she tried to picture the Doctor as a man – which she had been for over two thousand years. Knowing her now that just seemed silly. Although, it did explain one thing.

'That's why you call yourself a Time Lord, not a Time Lady,' Yaz muttered.

The Doctor had sharp ears. 'No, it's because "Time Lady" sounds like a watch you'd buy on the shopping channel.' Her hand shot out again. She waggled her fingers and said, 'Electron spanner.'

Not long after they'd returned the last of the former prisoners to their home world, Graham requested a visit to earth. He claimed he had to go back to water his houseplants, but Yaz suspected it was about more than a neglected yucca. Despite having been the keenest of all three to leave earth behind, he sometimes got very homesick.

So, a few weeks after they'd first left the planet, they arrived in Graham's front room. The geography was spot on, the chronology less so. Yaz had noted that the Doctor's piloting of the TARDIS was variable. Often they'd arrive in the right place, but at the wrong time – or vice versa.

While Ryan settled himself in the front room to catch up on some TV shows he'd missed, Yaz and the Doctor helped Graham sort through a deep pile of mail. Then Graham turned down the heating, watered the plants and popped next door to ask his neighbour to keep an eye on the place, spinning her a line about visiting relatives in Australia for a few months. The short visit seemed to be enough to satisfy him, and after a couple of hours he was ready to leave again.

'What's that?' Yaz asked when he returned to the TARDIS, pointing to the houseplant cradled in his arms.

'A begonia,' said Graham.

A piece of earth, thought Yaz. *In every sense.*

The Doctor was waiting for them in the console room. They found her sitting cross-legged on the floor, head buried in what looked like a glossy magazine, with dozens more littering the space around her and scattered over the central console. She poked her head over the top of the magazine.

'Group vote,' she said. 'Which one do we like best?'

Yaz picked up the nearest magazine and inspected its cover. 'It's a holiday brochure.'

'I thought after our recent excitement, we could all do with a spot of R and R,' the Doctor went on.

'I'm in,' said Graham. 'So long as it stands for what I think it does, and not something like Robots and Ravenous monsters.' He scooped up a brochure with a photograph on the front

24

of a beach with rainbow-coloured sand. 'What about this one?' He read from the description. 'Argolis, the Leisure Hive, offers –'

The Doctor plucked the brochure from his hand and tossed it over her shoulder. 'Been there. Had a few issues with their tachyon generator. Next.'

'Minehead?' suggested Ryan.

In the end, they decided on a planet called Lotos B – but as it turned out it was of no consequence, since they didn't ever get there.

And it was all because of Graham's begonia.

3. Re-potted

The TARDIS's wardrobe was lined with more racks than a department store but, unlike an earthly clothing shop, the fashions covered every time period imaginable, not to mention attire suitable for any number of alien weddings and birthday parties.

Graham was packing a case for the upcoming holiday and singing along to a playlist of seventies classics, which was being piped into the room by the TARDIS's rather fabulous – when it worked – sound system.

'Giver of Water,' squeaked a voice.

Graham ignored it, putting the high-pitched outburst down to the Bee Gees. He carried on with what he was doing, dangling two jumpers over his suitcase. It was a short break, and he knew he should only pack one, but, much as he might have liked to be, he just wasn't one of those carefree one-jumper people. What if there was an accident? What if there was spaghetti bolognaise? He packed both.

Just as he was picking up a third jumper, the voice squeaked again.

'Gray-ham, Giver of Water.'

That definitely wasn't the Bee Gees.

He spun round. The only thing near him, besides clothes of course, was his begonia, sitting on a low table. He'd taken to carrying the plant with him from room to room. He couldn't say exactly why, only that it reminded him of home, and perhaps of what he'd lost.

The dark green leaves rattled. How odd. He had been careful to position it away from any draughts.

Putting aside the jumper, he knelt down beside the plant so that he was at eye level with its largest flower. Immediately it unfurled, and turned to him like he was the sun.

'Gray-ham, Giver of Water,' said the plant. 'I have a message for the Doctor.'

*

Five minutes later, a still-astonished Graham stood with Yaz, Ryan and the Doctor in the console room. The talking houseplant sat on the floor before them, stubbornly silent. It hadn't spoken since Graham had rushed in with it from the wardrobe.

Ryan peered closely at it, then cast a doubtful expression at his granddad. 'You sure you weren't hearing things? I mean, at your age . . .'

'Cheeky little –'

'Shhh,' said the Doctor, clasping a leaf between her fingers and rubbing gently. 'They don't like raised voices. Or being moved. Give it a minute to adjust to its new environment, then I'm sure we'll hear what it has to say.' She smiled at the plant. 'Won't we?'

It remained silent.

'Does this happen a lot?' asked Graham in a low voice. 'I mean, messages coming via houseplants?'

'Highly efficient means of communication,' said the Doctor. 'Root systems run deep, pollen and seeds fly vast distances. Ever talked to a plant?'

Graham gave a sheepish nod. 'But it's the first time one's answered back.'

'That's the TARDIS,' said the Doctor. 'Its telepathic circuits are translating your plant's words into English.'

'But why does this begonia have a message for you?' asked Yaz.

'The plant is just the messenger,' said the Doctor. 'Someone else is using it to talk to me. The question is who?'

'And how did they know you'd be in my house?' asked Graham.

'They didn't,' said the Doctor. 'All the originator of the message had to do was plant the message somewhere on earth, then it travelled via the root network, seeking out its recipient. Probably find they've left the same message on lots of planets.' She gazed into the middle distance. 'I thought that orchid on Solaria was trying to get my attention.'

Unlike the others, Ryan was now keeping his distance, eyeing the houseplant warily from the back wall of the room.

'Why are you standing all the way over there?' said the Doctor.

Ryan blanched. 'In case it suddenly shoots out snake-like tendrils, wraps them round our throats, sticks them in our ears and takes control of our minds.'

'It's a begonia, Ryan, not a triffid.' She took a step back. 'Though, it could be a Krynoid ... Sarah Jane and I had a few problems with one of those.'

Yaz studied the Doctor's face. She was prone to these kinds of outbursts, referring to other travelling companions, other times. So many lives had passed through these TARDIS doors, Yaz reflected, and one day she, Ryan and Graham would leave too, just like the rest. She felt a tiny shiver.

The leaves of the begonia fluttered, and its stems straightened, as if the plant was stretching after a nap. The largest flower turned to face upwards.

'Doctor,' it declared. 'I bring greetings from the Gardeners of Tellus. They need your help, and request your presence on Tellus IV in order to brief you on a matter of great importance. The very existence of the universe is staked.'

'At stake,' corrected the Doctor.

'What did I say?' said the begonia.

'Never mind. Go on.'

The plant rustled its leaves. 'I have sent your vessel the planet's co-ordinates. With your permission, we should travel there immediately.'

'Yes, yes. Of course.' The Doctor stroked her chin. 'Gardeners of Tellus, eh? Interesting. Very interesting.' She ran to the circular console, pushed a handful of buttons, and jammed a lever or two from one position to another.

Ryan watched her carefully, as he did every time she piloted the TARDIS, trying to figure out the particular combination of switches, levers and dials that coaxed the vessel into motion. Despite paying close attention, he could never figure it out. If he was honest, it seemed she was making it up as she went along.

The familiar groaning and wheezing filled the console room. Ryan would never get over the feeling of travelling through space and time. Not that there was much actual sensation. One second they'd be in deep space, the next opening the police-box door on to an alien horizon (or Graham's front room). Occasionally, there'd be a patch of turbulence, but generally it was the smoothest, most unruffled travel he'd experienced – and he'd been in a Mercedes with AIRMATIC suspension. Ryan loved cars. Back on earth, he had wanted to be a mechanic, so from the moment he came aboard he'd quizzed the Doctor about the workings of the ship's engine.

'How much horsepower does this thing have?' had been his first question, as he tried to understand its capabilities in familiar terms.

'Don't know about that, but she'll do nought to sixty million years AD in eight seconds. Seven with a following solar wind.'

Ryan hadn't understood what that meant, but it sounded impressive, so he'd let out a long whistle. Then he'd stroked the bulkhead, sure he could feel a vibration like a heartbeat. 'How d'you even get one of these in the first place? Is there, like, a dealership?'

'You don't buy a TARDIS.'

'So it's leased?'

'A TARDIS is earned, rather than paid for.' The Doctor had looked sheepish. 'I, erm, borrowed this one.'

With a thud, the TARDIS settled, and the wheezing faded into silence. They had arrived.

'Tellus IV,' announced the Doctor. 'Well, come along.'

Without waiting for the others, she dashed outside, grinning like a kid at the start of the summer holidays. Yaz and Ryan followed, with Graham pausing only to collect his talking begonia before heading after them. Stopping in the doorway, dazzled by the glare of yet another alien sun, he let out a sigh.

'Here we go again.'

4. Gardeners' World

The planet smelled of freshly mown grass.

The TARDIS had landed atop a small hill at the edge of what looked to Ryan like one of the posh country estates from the period dramas his grandma Grace used to love watching on telly. In the distance, the windows of a great mansion with honey-coloured walls were glinting in the late-afternoon sunshine. Between the TARDIS and the house lay an ordered patchwork of green fields dotted with sheep, which gave way to a sweep of cropped lawn.

A stream flowed down from a ring of surrounding hills, draping across the landscape like a silver ribbon, then trickled through a small wood. Ryan didn't know the name of the trees, but they made a whispering sound when the breeze blew through their leaves. Beyond the wood, on another rise, sat a ruined tower like something out of a fairy tale.

As he gazed out at the picturesque landscape, Ryan felt his shoulders relax and he heard himself release a long breath.

Graham clearly didn't share Ryan's sense of ease. 'How do you know we're not walking into a trap?' he asked the Doctor.

'I don't.' She wiggled her eyebrows. 'Exciting, isn't it?'

She set off down the hill.

Graham silently appealed to the other two, but they just shrugged and followed the Doctor. He considered objecting, but knew it wouldn't do any good. The Doctor may have been over two thousand years old, but she had the impulse control of a teenager with their first credit card. Clutching his plant to his chest, he hurried after them.

'I feel like I've been here before,' said Yaz. 'But that's impossible.'

'You're remembering something buried deep inside you,' said the Doctor. 'Your home planet's not called earth for nothing. You lot have a special connection with the soil. What you're looking at, smelling, hearing, touching –' she stroked the long grass – 'all of this is in you.' She tapped a finger against Ryan's temple. 'Like a memory.'

Ryan was confused. 'But the Gardeners aren't from earth.'

'No, and they're not from this planet either. They spread out across the universe. Like seeds in the wind.'

They came to the beginning of a path constructed of mossy stepping stones. It curved alongside the stream, taking them towards the wood.

'The place didn't look like this when the first of them arrived. It was a hot, barren world, but they saw the potential. All it took was a fleet of transport ships loaded with topsoil from their home world, and patience. The Gardeners are some of the most patient people in the universe. I've met mountains in more of a hurry. They plant for the future – and not just for the next season, but for the next thousand. This whole planet is their garden.'

'Is it just me,' said Graham. 'Or is that mansion not getting any closer?'

'Well spotted, Graham,' said the Doctor. 'The house, like that ruin over there, is held in a perspective field, which means that no matter where you are in the landscape the view is always at its most agreeable.'

'Is it all like this?' asked Ryan. 'I mean, country houses and water features?'

'Oh no, you'll find every kind of garden imaginable. Some ordered and harmonious, others disordered and harmonious, walled gardens, wild gardens, zero-G gardens, hanging gardens, hanging baskets. And then there are the greenhouses: perfect, seamless domes, each stretching a kilometre across. The glasshouses of Tellus are one of the great architectural achievements of the galaxy. And wait till you try their tomatoes.'

The cool of the wood came as a relief after their stroll in the afternoon sun. They walked beneath trees hung with clusters of plump blue fruit the shape of peaches. The Doctor plucked several and handed them round.

'This place is like paradise,' said Yaz, taking a bite and wiping juice from her chin.

The Doctor made a face. 'Between you and me, Tellus is a bit boring. Plenty of life, but not much nightlife, if you know what I'm saying.' The Doctor stopped and held up a finger. 'One other thing. Over the millennia, the Gardeners have evolved into beings perfectly designed to tend the soil. Do not be alarmed.'

From up ahead came the splash of running water, and shortly after they arrived in a clearing. The stream they had been following ran down a rocky slope into a shady pool. At the edge waited three Gardeners, though it wasn't until they moved that the Doctor and the others noticed their presence, so well were they blended into their surroundings.

Each Gardener stood approximately ten feet tall, on gnarled, trunk-like legs with knees wide and padded for kneeling. They each had two long arms, one ending in a fork-shaped hand with tapering green fingers, the other like a pair of secateurs. Their faces were vaguely human, but instead of skin they were covered in green leaves. Branches curled round their heads, vines sprouted from their mouths, and insects wriggled across their wooded faces. From within the foliage of their faces gazed two large brown eyes, and their noses were twice the size of a human being's, with a flap over each nostril. *Maybe a pollen filter*, Graham speculated.

'Welcome to Tellus IV,' said the middle Gardener in a voice as deep as his roots. He bowed, creaking like a tree bending in the wind. 'Allow me to present *Convallaria majalis.*'

'Lily of the Valley,' said the Gardener to his left with what sounded like a tut. 'He likes using our Latin names when we have guests.'

Ignoring his colleague's objection, the middle Gardner gestured to the one on his right. 'And *Petroselinum crispum.*'

'Parsley,' the third Gardener clarified.

The middle Gardener then took a slow step forward. 'And my name is *Quercus robur,*' he said. 'You may call me Oak.'

'Right then,' said the Doctor, mimicking Oak's formal bow. 'Take us to your cedar.'

The leader of the Gardeners was not located in the mansion, but in a walled garden next to it. Her name was *Salix fragilis*, or Willow.

'You must be hungry after your journey,' she said, when the visitors arrived with the three Gardeners. She had laid on a formal meal, which took the form of a picnic on the grass.

Graham hesitated. How come wherever they went in the universe there was never a chair?

The picnic was a mixture of the familiar and the alien: rainbow-coloured grapes that sparkled in the sunshine, ripe figs that sighed with contentment when you bit into them, blushing strawberries that pulsed in the hand like living hearts. There were vegetable tarts and thick soups with crunchy croutons that never got soft, all washed down with a green and glutinous juice at once sharp and sweet. Around them, Gardeners tended to the plants and flowers. Bees buzzed in the herbaceous borders. Sunlight flickered through the sprinkle of watering cans.

'Your friend appears to be thirsty,' Parsley said to Graham.

'Doubt it,' said Graham, gesturing to Ryan. 'He's just downed a gallon of space cider.'

'Oh, not him,' said Parsley. 'Your plant.'

Graham looked down at the begonia by his side.

The plant aligned several leaves to point across the lawn at a Gardener emptying a watering can over a rose bush. 'I'll have what she's having,' it said.

As they ate, Willow revealed her reason for contacting the Doctor. 'What do you know of the Galactic Seed Vault?'

The Doctor bit into an apple. 'It was created to store and preserve examples of plant seeds from across the universe, so that in the event of planetary catastrophe or galactic apocalypse the seeds will survive to be replanted. But no one knows who's responsible for it. It's an MLITMOT.'

Parsley's bushy face curled in puzzlement. 'A what?'

'Mystery lost in the mists of time,' she explained. 'Yes, it's up there with the monoliths on the moons of Europa, and with Stonehenge. This is a great apple. Crunchy and tangy and sweet all at the same time. Might be the best apple I've ever tasted. Do you mind?' She reached for another, then decided to take all the remaining apples and stuff them in her pockets.

'One of our people created the vault,' announced Willow. '*Malus pumila*, also known as the First Gardener. She was aided in her endeavour by the Time Lords.'

The Doctor's hand froze midway to her pocket. 'Huh. You learn something new every regeneration. What were my lot doing there? We're not exactly the most green-fingered of races.'

'The Time Lords' role remains unknown,' said Willow. 'The First Gardener also attempted to hide her part, and nothing is written down in our histories. It is as if she wanted to forget what she had done. Yet a few of us know the vault's true origins, including one who goes by the name *Atropa belladonna*.'

'Deadly nightshade,' Graham chimed in. He had known those garden-centre catalogues would come in useful one day.

Willow nodded. 'He leads a faction that regards the vault as blasphemous. They hold extreme beliefs. In their view, no plant should be confined indoors; all should be under the sky. Nightshade and his insurgents have already laid waste to our greenhouses. Now they plan to destroy the vault itself.'

'Well, they won't succeed,' said the Doctor. 'The Galactic Seed Vault is on the ice planet of Calufrax Major. If the cold doesn't get them, the vault will. It's one of the most secure buildings in the universe.'

'Indeed, Doctor,' said Willow. 'But they are already inside. We have learned of a plan that was set in motion ten generations ago and is about to come to fruition. Thousands of years in our past, a single seed was collected by the vault-keepers. They did not know that it had been grown by Nightshade's predecessors and laid as a trap. Far from being an ordinary seed, it is a weapon, and now it lies at the heart of the seed vault, primed and ready. You must get to it first. Remove it before it germinates and destroys the vault and everything in it.'

'Why not just send a message to whoever's running the vault?' asked Yaz. 'Warn them about the bad seed and let them take care of it.'

'We have already done as you suggest. But there has been no response.'

The Doctor frowned. 'Now, don't get me wrong. I'm always happy to help out when there's an intergalactic mystery involved. But why wait for me? Why not go there yourselves?'

'Let me show you something,' said Willow, rising to her feet and gesturing for them to follow.

As she led them and the other Gardeners through a wooden door in one of the garden's mossy walls, they found themselves in a green maze with high walls of yew hedges.

'You are about to see something that no outsider has witnessed in forty generations,' Willow told them.

They smelled it before they saw it: a sweet, heady scent that drifted on the breeze. A moment later, they reached the centre of the maze and found it filled with roses.

'The Rose Garden of Eternity,' said Willow. 'The garden blooms but once every thousand years, with a prophecy written in its flowers.' She led them to a raised section, which offered a view of the whole garden. 'Behold.'

Yaz let out a gasp. The roses had flowered, forming pictures with their blooms. Picked out in blue was the distinctive shape of the TARDIS, and next to it a wedge-shaped building she assumed to be the Galactic Seed Vault. And, beneath both, in a profusion of colours was a number: '13'.

'We have been waiting for you, Doctor.' Willow turned to her. 'You are the Thirteenth Flowering.'

There was a rustle from the nearest hedge, and Graham's begonia let out a warning squeak. He looked round just in time to see a shrub detach itself from the yew hedge. It was just over six feet tall, with dense foliage and a gaping mouth full of thornlike teeth, and it scuttled towards them faster than any plant should move.

'Ambush!' cried Willow.

Too late, Graham saw another shrub creature moving out of the corner of his eye. This one was behind him but, as it reared its head to strike, Oak threw himself in the way. The attacker sank its thorny teeth into the Gardener's arm. He grimaced, before launching a counter-attack, using his secateurs hand to prune it mercilessly.

From overhead came the scream of engines. Out of the clear blue sky above the valley beyond appeared three silver scoop-shaped craft. The Tellus IV sun rolled off their curved wings as they dived, then adjusted their approach. Dropping low, the three craft tore across the valley, skimming the ridge, before forming up to commence their attack run. As the leader craft flew closer, the sunlight caught an insignia on its hull: a distinctive design consisting of bell-shaped purple flowers and dark berries.

'Nightshade,' muttered Willow, turning to the Doctor. 'He knows you are here. We have been betrayed.'

The airborne attackers were close enough now for them to see the doors open in the belly of the leading craft and disgorge a series of spherical projectiles.

'Seed bombs!' yelled Willow. 'Take cover!'

Guided by on-board systems, the bombs steered unerringly towards their targets. In the distance, the ruined folly exploded and the woodland burst into flames. The second ship released another salvo, and the ground shook with the impact.

In the maze, the Gardeners fought to fend off the ambush. Oak had taken care of one of the attackers and wore deep scratches on his arms to prove it, but that still left one more of the shrub creatures. It was just over half the height of the Gardeners, with a wide body made of woody stems interspersed with ropes of thorns, which it wielded as whips. It lashed out, and the whips cut through the air.

Willow dodged the first strike, ducked the follow-up, plunged her arm into the heart of the bush, then twisted her hand. There was a terrible snap and the creature sagged to the ground.

'They're coming back!' shouted Yaz, pointing at the sky.

The trio of attacking craft had reached the end of the valley, and were turning for another run. They swooped round in a tight manoeuvre, their razor-edged wings biting the air, but this time as they approached one of them peeled out of formation. There was the roar of retrorockets as it decelerated.

'It's coming in to land,' said Willow, a note of alarm in her voice. 'Doctor, you must leave.'

Moving swiftly to the rose bushes, Willow waved a hand over one section. The stems parted to reveal a hatch in the ground, which she lifted to expose steps leading downwards. She gestured to Lily of the Valley. 'Lead our guests to safety.'

Then she turned to the Doctor. 'Go now. Protect the seed vault!'

*

The silver craft came in for landing. Manoeuvring jets fired, and three stocky struts unfolded from its body. The rounded nose flared as the craft touched down on top of the maze, its exhaust blackening the foliage and its landing gear crushing the yew hedges.

Almost immediately a hatch opened in one side, and a ramp descended. Half a dozen Gardeners in green armour emerged, multi-barrelled weapons clasped in their gloved hands, their boots clattering as they came down the ramp. They fanned out, taking up defensive positions around the ship.

'Grave Diggers,' muttered Oak.

The soldiers' leaf armour was made from shade-tolerant forest leaves processed to become harder and lighter than Kevlar, while their weapons were customised black-ash branches designed to take a range of ammunition, including dieback rounds, creeper-shot and modified hemlock with poison-tipped thorns.

The Grave Digger commander signalled the all-clear.

A new figure appeared in the doorway. Taller than the rest, this Gardener had to stoop to clear the doorway. Once outside the craft, he straightened himself up and cast a lordly eye over his new surroundings. Unlike his personal guard of Grave Diggers, he was unarmoured. Instead, he was in full bloom, with a bandolier across his chest of bell-shaped purple flowers and shiny black berries that echoed the insignia painted on the hull of his ship. Belladonna. Deadly Nightshade.

Next to the rose garden, Willow, Oak and Parsley waited patiently.

As the leader of the breakaway faction approached, flanked by his troops, Parsley bolted forward and knelt before him. He grasped one of Nightshade's large hands, kissing it humbly.

'I have done your bidding, oh, great perennial. I sent the signal the moment the visitors arrived.'

Willow and Oak exchanged a look. The traitor had been among them all along.

Nightshade's voice was cool. 'You let them escape.'

'I did everything I could,' Parsley said, with a tremble of fear in his voice.

'And, yet, you failed me.' Nightshade paused. 'Take him to the compost heap.'

'No!' Parsley desperately grasped Nightshade's hand. 'By all that's herbaceous, please, no!'

Two Grave Diggers grabbed Parsley's arms, wresting his hands free from where he still clung to Nightshade, before dragging him away to his fate.

As Parsley's shrieks receded, Nightshade turned to Oak and Willow. 'You should not have involved the Time Lord.'

'Her role was predestined,' replied Willow.

'Ah, yes. The Rose Garden of Eternity.' Nightshade looked past her to the flowering display. 'A thorn in my side.' He nodded curtly to the Grave Digger nearest to him.

Unlike the black-ash blasters wielded by his comrades, this soldier wore a backpack connected by a long stem to a fat sunflower. He stepped towards the edge of the rose garden and levelled the yellow flower at the blooming roses.

'No!' Willow stepped forward to meet him. 'You cannot do this!'

But the surrounding Grave Diggers pinned both her and Oak's arms, holding them back. There was nothing they could do but watch as a flame leaped from the broad sunflower, and the soldier swept the spitting bloom from side to side, setting the entire garden ablaze. The eternal roses crackled and burned.

Nightshade surveyed the flames in quiet satisfaction. 'After the harvest comes the fire. All will be renewed in time. The soil must be turned.'

Snapping to attention, the Grave Diggers echoed him. 'The soil must be turned.'

5. Non Compost Mentis

'A little R and R, you said.' Using his thumb and forefinger, Graham prised a large thorn from his jumper. 'Remind me never to go on holiday with you again.'

The Doctor, meanwhile, was consulting the TARDIS database. 'Planet of Calufrax Major, polar region,' she said, entering the co-ordinates of the Galactic Seed Vault into the navigation computer. 'Narnia, here we come.'

Graham winced. 'Tell me we're not haring halfway across the galaxy because of a best-kept-village floral display.'

'The Rose Garden of Eternity doesn't make mistakes,' said the Doctor. 'It accurately predicted the great Mars ash dieback of 3004, the first and second Venus flytrap massacres, and the bee invasion of earth in 2151 AD.'

The console room filled with the familiar wheezing that indicated the TARDIS was on the move.

'And, c'mon, if I ignored an ancient mystical prophecy written in flowers, what kind of Time Lord would that make me?'

'As much as I hate to agree with Graham –' Ryan began.

'Cheers for that,' his granddad interrupted.

'This is pretty much the opposite of a holiday,' he finished. 'Anyway, what about that Nightshade character? Did you see those attack craft? They looked a bit like flying trowels, but they were packing some serious firepower. We're not equipped to go up against someone like that.'

'Trust me,' said the Doctor, 'they weren't as well armed as the seed vault is.' An alarm went off and she silenced it with the slap of a switch. 'We can't get too close, or we'll risk triggering ground-to-air defences –'

'What does a glorified garden centre need anti-aircraft blasters for?' Graham muttered.

'So we'll have to park and ride.' The Doctor pulled a lever and her fingers fluttered over the console, keying a sequence of buttons.

'Oh, come on,' Ryan complained, watching her. 'It's different *every* time.'

'There! That should set us down outside the danger zone. Calufrax Major isn't far from Tellus, so we'll arrive shortly.' She looked round at the others. 'But it is one of the coldest spots in the universe. I suggest you all wrap up warm.'

They set about preparing for their excursion. Graham decided to leave his begonia in the TARDIS, figuring that an ice planet was no place for a houseplant. He felt bad at first, worried it would get lonely without anyone to talk to, but the plant reassured him it would be just fine.

While Yaz filled a thermos flask with tea, Ryan headed off to the cavernous wardrobe, where he searched the racks for suitable outerwear. Spotting a multicoloured scarf, he plucked it off its hanger. *This will be perfect*, he thought – but, as he started to uncoil it, he found it just kept on coming. The scarf was endless, as if it had been knitted by some possessed grandma. *An obvious trip hazard.* He returned it to the rack.

Once he'd collected enough suitable kit, he returned to the console room and found Graham waiting there. The two of them rigged themselves out in polarised goggles, gloves, warm coats with furry hoods, windproof trousers and insulated boots. They were ready.

'Where are Yaz and the Doc?' asked Graham, his voice slightly muffled by the high fur collar of his coat.

He was answered by a slithering sound that came from just beyond the wardrobe door. In unison, he and Ryan looked nervously towards the door . . .

A moment later, the two women appeared, each hauling a wooden sledge and carrying what looked like a set of reins. Graham and Ryan breathed a sigh of relief.

Yaz stopped and stared at the two of them, swaddled in their snow gear. 'You look like a couple of yetis.'

'You never told me that you'd met the Yetis!' The Doctor was beaming at Yaz. 'I remember them well. Cuddly, but fierce. Robots, of course . . .'

While the Doctor finished her Yeti story, she and Yaz also donned cold-weather outfits, just in time for the TARDIS to land. With an enormous mitten-clad hand, the Doctor pawed the door-control lever. The mechanism whined, but the doors remained shut.

'Must be frozen,' she said.

'But we just got here a second ago,' said Graham. 'How cold *is* this planet?'

'This should help.' The Doctor hit a switch. 'De-icer.' She tried the doors again.

This time they opened smoothly, but Graham immediately wished they hadn't. A blast of freezing air hit him, collecting around his hood and turning the fake fur into icicles. Already shivering, he followed the Doctor, Yaz and Ryan as they dragged the sledges out of the TARDIS.

They found themselves on a wide, snowy plateau. For a moment, Ryan wondered if they'd been turned into fish fingers and materialised inside a freezer cabinet. As his eyes adjusted to the glare, he was able to see beyond their immediate surroundings. The white plateau stretched for miles in every direction, an unbroken, featureless expanse that eventually met a distant range of mountains, rows of jagged peaks gnawing at the indigo sky. He could see something at the base of the tallest mountain. From this distance it was no more than a smudge, but Ryan could fix that. He lifted a small pair of binoculars he'd found in the TARDIS wardrobe to his eyes. They were made of brass, with an odd handle and poor magnification, but they'd do.

'I wondered where those'd got to,' said the Doctor. 'Haven't seen them since the premiere of *The Magic Flute*. Wolfgang gave them to me.'

'Wolfgang?' said Graham. 'As in Mozart?'

'A thank-you gift.' She shrugged. 'I helped him with a little haunted-mask problem.'

Ryan pointed out the distant object to the others. Through the binoculars, he could see it was a black, angular building that jutted from the bottom of the mountain like a giant's step. 'If that's where we're headed,' he said. 'It's going to be a long walk.'

'Who said anything about walking?' The Doctor held up her sonic screwdriver.

As with the TARDIS, Ryan was fascinated by the sonic. From what he'd observed, the Doctor used it mostly to open doors. But, while it was sophisticated enough to unlock or manipulate most kinds of technology, for some reason it had no effect whatsoever on wood. Ryan couldn't believe no one had come up with a setting for that. He suspected that it was only called a sonic screwdriver for the – *whatchamacallit?* – alliteration.

'Hear that?' said the Doctor.

Ryan shook his head.

'That's because you're not a Frost Lepus. I'm using the sonic to send out a high-frequency signal. Bit like a dog whistle.'

Aha! So, it does use sound energy, Ryan mentally noted with interest.

'Uh, what's that?' Graham was squinting at a trail of tracks that stretched across the white landscape. 'Shouldn't we get back to the TARDIS?' he asked nervously.

The Doctor waved a dismissive mitten. 'Relax. They're perfectly friendly. Just so long as you don't act like a carrot.'

Before he could question the Doctor, Graham saw four rabbit-like creatures bounding across the snow towards them. They came to a stop in front of the Doctor, panting in the cold air. Sitting on their haunches they were as tall as Graham, and had white furry coats, two black button eyes and a small pink nose that never stopped twitching, as if it was always on the point of sneezing.

The Doctor looped her makeshift harness round two of them, then tethered it to one of the sledges. Yaz did the same, and then sat down at the back of her sledge. She beckoned to Ryan to join her, while the Doctor shared her sledge with Graham.

'So this is what you meant by park and ride?' said Ryan.

'More like park and leap,' said Yaz, as the Frost Lepuses pawed impatiently at the ground.

'Are you sure this is safe?' Graham looked uncertain.

'Statistically speaking, there's no safer way to travel,' the Doctor reassured him. 'I mean, how many people do you know who've been injured or killed travelling on a sledge pulled by giant bunnies?' Before Graham could answer, she snapped the reins. 'Hold on!'

Yaz followed suit. Sitting behind the loping creatures as they hauled the sledge along, she felt filled with happiness. As a kid, she'd begged for a pet rabbit but, her dad being allergic to animal fur, she hadn't been allowed one.

'Mister Hoppy,' she said aloud, remembering the cuddly toy she'd made do with instead.

Ryan frowned. 'Come again?'

'Nothing.' Yaz was grateful for the hood, which hid her blush.

'Can I drive?' asked Ryan.

'No.'

Flattening their ears, the Lepuses picked up speed across the snowy plain. With sure-footed ease, they dodged deep drifts and leaped crevasses, bearing their exhilarated passengers towards their destination.

After some time, they came within the long shadow of the mountains. Through the reins, Yaz could feel the Lepuses begin to slow and grow skittish the nearer they drew to the vault, until eventually the creatures refused to go any further. Thankfully, the vault was near enough to proceed on foot, so the Doctor released the Lepuses from their harnesses, and they set out on the final leg of their journey. By the time they reached the outskirts of the vault, night was falling and, with it, the temperature. Yaz found it hard to believe the place could get any colder.

Before them lay the Galactic Seed Vault: a bluff, wedge-shaped building constructed of some kind of light-sucking material, approximately fifty metres across and rising 200 metres straight up into the darkening sky – and who knew how deep it reached into the mountain itself. Freezing winds shrieked across its blank face, complaining at the angular obstruction.

'Strange,' said the Doctor. 'I would have expected a welcoming committee by now. A warning laser-shot, a sonic blast, a pack of robot guard dogs . . .'

But avoiding the vault's active defences was the least of Ryan's concerns. With growing anxiety, he saw that in order to reach the building they would have to cross a chasm on a narrow metal bridge with no guardrail. A challenge for most people, this would be doubly difficult for him, as he suffered from dyspraxia – a disorder that meant he often struggled with movement and co-ordination, which could make physical tasks extra challenging. He looked at the bridge. A mere stumble would prove fatal. Then, assuming he could even make it across, another obstacle remained on the opposite side: there was no door.

The lack of an entrance didn't seem to bother the Doctor, though. 'We must tread carefully from here,' she was saying. 'Visitors aren't permitted in case of contamination, so we will be the first people to enter the seed vault since its construction.' She thought for a moment. 'Actually, that's not strictly accurate. I did hear of an attempt to rob the vault of some of its rarer specimens several thousand years ago. Four plant-hunters were hired by a collector to source the seeds for his private garden. They apparently made it past the first level of security, but no further.'

'What happened to them?' asked Yaz.

'Several months later, four pots of compost were delivered to their home worlds. Upon analysis, the contents were identified as the remains of the plant-hunters.' She paused. 'It's what they would've wanted.'

'It's not what I want!' Graham objected.

'Any idea how they got in?' asked Yaz. 'Before they were, um, composted.'

'You could use your sonic,' Ryan suggested.

'No need,' said the Doctor. 'If I've timed it correctly – which I have – then . . .'

She looked up into the sky just as what appeared to be a comet entered the planet's atmosphere. It was low on the horizon and burned brightly in the darkness. Changing direction, it angled towards them.

'Uh, what is that?' asked Graham.

'A seed-collecting drone,' said the Doctor. 'I asked the TARDIS to locate one as soon as we left Tellus IV. This one's been out in the universe for a thousand years, searching for a single seed, and now it's coming home.'

There was a series of dull, metallic clunks, then a horizontal seam appeared in the face of the vault at the end of the bridge. It split in two, each half rolling back. As the gap widened, the seed-collecting drone shot over their heads. It was moving slowly now, on its final approach, and they could see that it was the size of a bird. Retrorockets engaged as the vessel manoeuvred itself through the gap.

'Quickly now, before the doors close again. We can't afford to hang around for another thousand years.'

The Doctor hurried across the bridge, and the others dashed after her.

Ryan reached the middle of the bridge before he froze. The wind wailed up from the depths of the chasm and swirled around the flimsy bridge, causing it to buck and creak. He watched the others reach the opposite side. Yaz and the Doctor kept going, but Graham paused, noticing Ryan's absence. He turned round and saw his grandson.

'It's okay,' he called through the wind. 'Looks more dangerous than it is. I'll help you.'

He began to make his way back towards Ryan, but no sooner had he set foot on the bridge than his feet went out from under him. He hit the slick metal surface and, with a yell, slid towards the edge.

There was nothing else for it. Ryan dived full length across the bridge.

'Got you!' He grabbed Graham by the sleeve of his puffy coat and hauled him up, and together they made their way safely to the other side. Up ahead, the Doctor and Yaz stood at the entrance to the vault, peering back through the snow for their friends. Ryan gave them a wave, and the two women disappeared inside.

'Couldn't have been dyslexia, could it?' grumbled Graham.

Ryan gave his granddad a wry smile. To think that just a few months ago they'd been at home on earth worrying about him catching a bus or passing an exam, and now here they were, dicing with death over an alien abyss. They looked at one another, silently marvelling at the sheer improbability of their new life, but their relief at this latest narrow escape was cut short by a clang that split the wind.

The doors of the seed vault had ground shut.

They were alone in the frozen night.

'We have to get the doors open again!' Yaz hammered her gloved fists against the unyielding surface. 'They'll freeze to death out there.'

The Doctor had already raised her sonic screwdriver. 'We'll get them back. Don't worry.' The device glowed as she passed it back and forth across the space where the doors had been.

'They're not opening,' said Yaz, trying to quell her rising panic.

'Must be wood in the structure. Y'know what? I don't think this building was constructed. It was grown. How fascinating.'

'Not the time, Doctor.' Yaz looked around desperately for some sort of control panel. She figured that the two men would be okay for a while, but there was no way they could last the night outside, and it was too far for them to make it back to the TARDIS on foot – even if they could have found their way in the dark.

Yaz's breath plumed in front of her. The temperature in here was barely higher than outside, but at least she and the Doctor were out of that wind and they were dry – which was more than she could say for Ryan and Graham.

Yaz scoured every surface in her search. As she moved round the room, she guessed this must be the drone hangar. A launch-and-retrieval bay from which the seed-collecting drones were sent out into the galaxy to return months, years – thousands of years – later with their precious cargo.

The retrieval section was at the far end, a covered conveyor belt loaded with glass spheres. They were small enough to fit in a human palm, and on closer inspection Yaz saw that each contained a single tiny seed. The conveyor belt was clearly intended to shuttle the seeds to another part of the vault. However, the belt was still, gathering dust. *Strange.* More importantly, given the current urgency of their situation, the bay appeared to be sealed off from the rest of the vault. The only way to pass deeper into the vault seemed to be along the conveyor belt, but that was enclosed in a sealed transparent tunnel.

'There must be a control room somewhere else in this place,' said Yaz, frantically racing through their limited options. 'We can open the main doors from there, but we need to find a way into the rest of the vault.'

She turned to find the Doctor with her ear pressed to the back wall, moving slowly along its length and talking to herself. 'Yes. Grown, not built. Like a shell. Sea, not turtle, obviously. Cells secrete a protein matrix, which binds calcium ions and encourages calcification. She sells seashells on the seashore. She sells seashells on the sea–'

The Doctor stopped abruptly, took a pace back and aimed a kick at a point on the wall. The blow was enough to loosen a layer of dust, which fell away to reveal the partial outline of a door. Removing a mitten, she ran a finger round an emerging frame. It clearly hadn't been opened in a very long time. The doorway was wider than it was tall, designed for something beyond human proportions.

This was it: their way into the rest of the vault. But there was no obvious handle, keypad or lock.

With a click, the door began to slide open.

'How did you do that?' asked Yaz.

'I didn't,' said the Doctor. 'I'm guessing he did.'

In front of them, filling the doorway with its bulk, crouched a beetle-like creature. It was making a furious chittering noise, and the mandibles on either side of its head twitched alarmingly. Yaz watched in horror as it reached for the Doctor with one of its multi-segmented forelegs, the claw on the end snipping the air.

'Doctor!'

6. The Curatrix

'I'm the Doctor and this is Yaz,' said the Doctor, standing her ground before the advancing beetle. 'We're here to help.'

'I don't think it understands you,' Yaz cautioned.

'Our friends are outside the vault,' the Doctor continued regardless. 'They'll freeze to death if we don't open the door for them. Can you do that?' The beetle carried on, forcing the Doctor to back away. 'We won't hurt you. The Gardeners of Tellus sent us. I'm in a prophecy . . .'

Yaz saw that the Doctor's words were having no effect, as the beetle continued to chitter and snap at her. A more robust response was needed. While Yaz had some training in hand-to-hand combat, she wasn't convinced it would be of much use against a giant insect opponent. Perhaps the Doctor was better equipped. 'Hope you know some space karate?'

'Venusian aikido,' said the Doctor. 'A more subtle martial art, favoured by a few of us Time Lords.'

The beetle came to a sudden stop, its attacking posture giving way to a more passive stance.

'I think it *does* understand you,' said Yaz. 'When you said–'

'Time Lord.' The Doctor and the beetle were nose-to-proboscis. 'From the planet Gallifrey. Distantly related to those who helped create this Galactic Seed Vault.'

The beetle stepped back, and then made a strangely human beckoning motion with its claw. It swung round and plodded off through the doorway it had entered from, down a long, dark passageway.

'I think it wants us to follow it,' said the Doctor. 'Seems friendly enough.'

Yaz's relief at finally communicating their peaceful intentions to the beetle was immediately replaced by uneasiness at heading after it into the unknown. However, she knew that if they were to have any hope of rescuing Ryan and Graham she had to go along.

As they followed their strange guide, their presence triggered temporary lighting. Sections of the wall glowed as they approached, fading again as soon as they'd passed. They were a moving bubble of light in the darkness.

'Bioluminescence,' mused the Doctor. 'Light produced by a living organism. It can sense we're here.'

'Are you saying this building is alive?'

'Quite possibly,' she replied, a shadow crossing her face. 'And I don't think it's feeling too well.'

'What do you mean?'

'The vault has a reputation for being one of the most impregnable buildings in the universe. A death trap to the uninvited. And yet we swanned inside without so much as breaking a sweat.'

Yaz bridled at the Doctor's description of how easy it had been. They were, after all, two men down.

'Something is wrong here,' the Doctor went on. 'Very wrong.'

Before Yaz could quiz her further, they came to a transit station at which a capsule-shaped vehicle large enough to accommodate a handful of passengers waited: the vault's internal transport system. The beetle climbed through a low, open hatch in one side of the capsule, and the Doctor and Yaz stooped to follow it. Since the vehicle was not designed for humans, there were no seats inside. Yaz found a rail to cling to, as the hatch whirred shut, then with a seamless surge of power they sped off.

They spent a few seconds in a tunnel, before they burst with a *whoosh* out into what Yaz at first thought must be the outside, so vast was the space. Then she looked up through the transparent canopy and realised that what she'd believed to be a sky full of stars was in fact light reflecting on the underside of a distant ceiling.

They were travelling through one of the seed storage vaults.

Pillars of glass hundreds of metres high rose up out of the vault floor, and the transport capsule weaved in and out of the crystalline forest they formed. As the capsule skirted close to one of the pillars, Yaz gasped. It was formed of countless spherical seed jars just like the ones she'd seen in the hangar bay.

They picked up speed again, passing through a patch of criss-crossing beams of light. Yaz realised that the beams were caused by strange firefly-like insects flitting from one section of the vault to another. The flying bugs were using their lights to inspect each seed jar and ensure that it was in perfect working order, keeping its precious contents at the ideal temperature.

They passed through a connecting corridor into the next vault, where a handful of fat green shoots slithered like pythons across the nearest wall.

'That shouldn't be here,' said the Doctor immediately.

Yaz was about to ask why not, when their transport capsule shot out from behind one of the glass towers to reveal the rest of the vault. She lifted a hand to her mouth in shock.

Half of the towers in this vault had been toppled, and countless seed jars lay shattered on the floor. More of the invasive shoots wound their way round the remaining fragile towers. It would be only a matter of time before they fell too.

Yaz gaped at the devastation. 'What happened?'

'The renegade Gardeners' time bomb,' said the Doctor. 'It's already detonated. We're too late.'

There was the wail of an alarm as the transport capsule's automatic collision-avoidance systems kicked in and it swerved to avoid a massive chunk of wall falling from above. In front of them, another section of wall crumbled away to expose the snake-like shoots throbbing beneath like veins.

Leaving the damaged vault behind, they passed through a connecting chamber and into the next vault. It too had been ravaged by the same choking weeds. They passed through wrecked vault after wrecked vault – Yaz counted half a dozen more – until finally the transport capsule dipped towards an exit barely bigger than its own dimensions and blasted into another tunnel. Yaz felt the air pressure build in her ears, and then the press of decelerating forces. They touched down, and the side hatch swung open.

'I think we've arrived,' said the Doctor.

They got out of the capsule, and found themselves in front of another squat door. Their beetle escort stood to one side and chittered again. With a whir, the door opened on to total darkness. Without hesitating, the Doctor stepped through but, as Yaz went to follow, the beetle scuttled in front of her, blocking her path.

'One at a time, I think,' said the Doctor, pausing to squeeze Yaz's hand. 'Don't worry.'

'I'm not worried,' said Yaz. There was something about the Doctor's presence that made even the most drastic situation bearable. She waited while the Doctor proceeded into the next room. A humming noise emanated from beyond, and she glimpsed flashes of light. Thirty seconds later, it was her turn.

She passed through the doorway into a small, circular chamber with opaque walls. With the same hum she'd heard before, a broad fan of red light appeared and, starting at her feet, moved slowly up her body. As she let the light wash over her, she couldn't help but reflect on the grim fate of the plant-hunters the Doctor had mentioned. If this was a composting death ray, she hoped it would all be over quickly.

Not a death ray, she decided after a few seconds. *But some kind of scan, perhaps searching for weapons.* The Doctor didn't approve of weapons, and the only item Yaz had on her was the thermos flask of tea. The red light dazzled her as it reached eye level, then it turned green. Surely a good sign – unless green had a different significance on this planet. Yaz held her breath.

The wall of the chamber revolved, then opened up to reveal a brightly lit room beyond. Yaz allowed herself to relax, if only for a moment, before she stepped into what was unquestionably a control room. No clutter of buttons, switches or levers; just a central pillar topped with a display, sitting at the heart of a circular white space. The display showed an image of a section of the seed vault, presumably fed to it by a camera. Every few seconds the image changed, as it switched to another camera feed.

The Doctor was already standing in front of the display, and was shuffling through the various feeds by waving her hands at the floating screen.

'Can you see Ryan and Graham?' Yaz asked, coming to stand beside her.

The Doctor switched the view so that the image became dark with spots of blue and green and white. 'I'm using the infrared setting to scan for their heat signatures,' she explained, as a couple of blurry human shapes bloomed on the screen. 'There!'

It was the two men. They had moved away from the entrance, presumably in search of another way in. Yaz and the Doctor had no means of contacting them, but at least they could see that they were okay – for now.

The beetle joined them in the control room. Yaz turned to it and said, 'I know you can understand me. You have to open the door and let them inside.'

No sooner had she finished than the air warped in front of them and a figure materialised. At first it took on an insectoid shape, before cycling through a series of transformations, until it finally settled on a humanoid form. Specifically, a strikingly tall woman with jet-black hair in a pinned-up bun. It wore dark trousers and a white high-collared shirt that was buttoned all the way up. In its long, elegant fingers it held a clipboard.

'I am the Curatrix,' it said flatly, its eyes suddenly burning red. 'And you are trespassing.'

7. Gardeners of
the Galaxy

Ryan pulled his coat closer round him and shivered. He reckoned they had another hour out here, max, before they turned into human popsicles. When it was clear that the vault's main entrance wouldn't be opening again any time soon, he and Graham began to seek another way in. He ran his gloved hand across the surface, noting its perfect smoothness. If there was another entrance, it was well concealed.

There was a boom from above. Ryan glanced into the night sky and saw a bright light. He felt a surge of hope that it might be another seed-collecting drone returning to the vault, before he recognised it as the fiery glow of an engine belonging to an atmospheric craft. It appeared they weren't the only visitors to Calufrax Major today.

High above, the craft began to circle towards the ground, buffeted by the turbulent mountain winds. As it came closer, Ryan saw that it was scoop-shaped like the three craft that had attacked them on Tellus IV. Could it be one of them? The Doctor had said it wasn't far between Tellus IV and here, so it was possible – especially if the Gardeners possessed faster-than-light travel, which seemed a good bet. From what Ryan had seen, for a race who on the face of it liked nothing better than to mow the lawn, Gardener technology was highly advanced.

The Doctor had been concerned about the vault's air defences, but as Ryan watched the silver craft come in to land it was clear that any defences must be down. A light flared on the underside of the ship, illuminating the ground at the same time as the familiar insignia on the hull: it was Nightshade's personal craft. It made a pass over the ridge, then set down on a flat section of ground between the chasm and the front of the vault.

The touch of a hand on Ryan's shoulder made him jump. Instinctively, he grabbed it and spun round to tackle the attacker. It was Graham. Before Ryan could protest that he shouldn't creep up on people like that, Graham gestured to the ship. The two of them dropped flat on to their bellies to avoid being spotted, then crawled across the ground and positioned themselves for a better view.

A hatch opened in the silver craft, and its occupants trooped out. Three armed Gardeners in some kind of leaf armour came first, followed by a taller figure with a criss-cross of purple flowers on his chest. This had to be the infamous rebel they'd been told about.

One of the armoured Gardeners lumbered to a spot about ten metres from the door, carrying what looked like a rocket launcher. He came to a stop and dug his heels into the snow. Ryan watched in amazement as roots grew rapidly out of his legs, pushing down through the frozen soil to anchor him in place. The Gardener then slung his weapon across his shoulder and took aim. There was a dull *whump* as it fired, and a moment later a projectile impacted against the door. The weapon wasn't explosive, but organic – a creeper that spread its vines across the face of the vault with alarming speed. Once it had spidered all the way out to the corners, there was a crack, and the massive door shattered into fragments. The armoured Gardener's roots then retracted into his legs, and he plodded after his comrades, who were already marching inside.

'We have to follow them,' said Ryan. 'The Doctor and Yaz are in there, and they have no idea what's coming.'

'Are you crazy?' Graham said. 'Did you see what they did to that door?'

'Well, it's either that or freeze to death out here.'

Graham muttered darkly, clearly unhappy with either option.

'Remember that mysterious dent in your car door?' Ryan said, and Graham's expression turned to one of confusion. 'Yeah, it was me. I borrowed your car without asking. I wanted to impress Alison Mayer, and I pranged it trying to buy her a drive-through burger.'

'Why are you telling me this now?'

'Because I figure you can't get more upset than you already are.' With that, Ryan got to his feet and padded towards the open vault.

The giant beetle's legs tap-tap-tapped on the smooth control-room floor, and its mandibles twitched alarmingly.

Yaz whirled around. *This is it*, she thought. *Any second now. Compost time.*

She backed away, but in her haste she bumped into the Curatrix – except that she didn't. Although the Curatrix appeared to be solid, Yaz passed right through it. She gave the Doctor a quizzical look.

'A holographic avatar of the artificial intelligence that runs this place,' the Doctor explained. 'An unimaginably powerful being. We must be careful.'

The image stuttered and wobbled, as if the signal generating it was losing strength. The beetle chittered again.

'I think it's talking to her,' Yaz said in a low voice.

'Time Lord?' said the Curatrix at last, turning to the Doctor.

'It's a pleasure to meet you, Curatrix,' the Doctor said with a courteous neck-bow. 'I saw the damage to the vaults and I'd like to help.'

The image steadied briefly. Yaz could tell that the Curatrix was making up its gigantic mind about whether to trust the Doctor. Thankfully, the AI was smart enough to know it was talking to an ally.

'You cannot help,' said the Curatrix. 'A rogue seed has already infected the facility – a modified variety of noughtweed from the planet Gehenna Prime.'

The screen in the centre of the room displayed an image of the same boa-constrictor-like shoots Yaz and the Doctor had seen in the vaults.

A pained expression came over the Doctor's face. 'Noughtweed is unstoppable. It's outlawed on every civilised world.'

'But it's just a weed, right?' said Yaz. 'Not some terrible biological weapon.'

'It eats biological weapons for breakfast.'

'I have conducted a full-spectrum analysis,' said the Curatrix. 'The weed has been modified in several notable ways.'

The image on the screen changed to show an annotated diagram of the weed's structure.

'Is that a time propagator?' The Doctor looked puzzled. 'Why does it need one of those?'

'Eight vaults are already damaged beyond repair,' the Curatrix went on. 'It is only a matter of time until the rest succumb.'

Yaz felt a spike of anger towards the rogue Gardeners who had caused this. 'They say they treasure all plant life,' she said. 'But, by destroying the seed vault, they'll wipe out millions of species of plants. It doesn't make any sense.'

The Doctor paused. 'Unless that isn't their ultimate plan.'

'What do you mean?'

She tapped her top lip in thought. 'Noughtweed is a random weapon, spreading indiscriminately wherever it can find something to get its hooks into. But, as the Curatrix has determined, this variety has been altered. See here.' She pointed to the display in the centre of the room, which now showed live images of the various vaults. 'Look at how the creepers are aligned. That's not nature; that's programming. Whoever created this variety of noughtweed didn't simply want to destroy – they wanted to *search* and destroy. The question is: what's the weed searching for?'

Still talking, she began to pace around the room.

'Willow told us that Nightshade regards the vault as a prison. What if he's after one prisoner in particular?' She spun round to address the Curatrix. 'How many seeds are stored here?'

There was a millisecond pause as the Curatrix accessed the most up-to-date records in the database. 'There are eight-hundred-and-thirty billion varieties of plant in seed form stored in this facility.'

'And how many individual vaults?'

'Twelve.'

In the corner of the room the beetle began tap-tapping one leg on the floor in a broken rhythm. Yaz studied it carefully. She didn't know anything about giant beetle body language, but she'd had enough experience of interviewing petty criminals to know that it was guilty about something.

Muttering to herself, the Doctor resumed her circling, deep in thought. A few seconds later, she came to a sudden stop, clapping her hands together.

'Can you show me a schematic of the seed vault?' she asked the Curatrix, who instantly produced a layout of the facility on screen.

The Doctor cast her eyes over the blueprint and shook her head. 'Nothing. Show me an older plan.'

'That is the oldest in my records,' the Curatrix replied.

In the silence that followed the only sound was the nervous tap-tap of the beetle's leg.

The Doctor raised an eyebrow. 'But is it?' She whipped out her sonic screwdriver and, activating it, swept the device across the Curatrix. 'Apologies for this, but I don't think you can voluntarily tell me what I need to know.'

The generated image of the Curatrix flickered and changed. The stern-looking humanoid woman disappeared. Only an outline remained, containing hundreds of lines of scrolling computer code.

'Unauthorised access attempt,' announced the Curatrix's voice. 'Unauthorised access att–' The Curatrix broke off, and when it spoke again the voice was the same, but the message had altered. 'Access granted.'

'Show me the original seed vault plans,' the Doctor instructed.

There was a short delay before a new layout appeared. Strikingly different from the previous set, these plans were displayed on yellowing parchment and appeared to be hand-drawn, like something Leonardo da Vinci might have included in one of his notebooks.

'What, exactly, are you looking for?' asked Yaz.

'The rose garden's prophecy was accurate, but the Gardeners misinterpreted the message.' Holding her sonic like a pointer, the Doctor indicated a portion of the plan. 'Count them: ten, eleven, twelve . . . thirteen.' She zoomed in. 'You see, the number in the garden didn't refer to me. It's the thirteenth vault. Not found on any other plan.'

'A secret vault!' Yaz realised. 'Cool.'

'And I'd bet a box of the finest Judoon chocolates that's where we'll discover the true target of this attack.'

The image flickered again and the Curatrix reappeared, refilling the outline. 'Impossible,' it said. 'I have no knowledge of a thirteenth vault.'

The Doctor tutted. 'But the Gardeners do. Now, what could possibly be in there that the creators of this place didn't want even their guardian AI to know about? Unless, that is, you're not the only guardian . . .' She swung round to peer at the beetle.

'Doctor,' said a voice full of hisses and clicks.

It took Yaz a moment to realise she hadn't heard the voice out loud, but in her head. It was another second before she understood it was coming from the beetle.

The insect's mandibles clicked furiously. 'Thirteen must be contained.'

8. Cuppa Tea?

The transport capsule lifted off with the beetle in the front.

Yaz pulled her coat around her and felt the solid shape of her thermos flask in the inside pocket. As much as she could have done with one right now, there wasn't time for a cup of tea. She and the Doctor found handrails to cling on to, as the creature wheeled the vessel tightly round then blasted on through the connecting tunnel and into the adjoining seed vault.

'Doctor,' Yaz said. 'I heard it . . . in my mind. Was that telepathy?'

The Doctor nodded. 'Quite common among insectoid races. They tend to operate as a hive mind, communicating as one. Can be rather tiresome, to be honest. You get to hear a lot of chatter about compound eyes and larvae and who has the shiniest wings. This one seems perfectly adapted to its environment, though. My guess is it was engineered by the Gardeners who created the vault to be part of the whole system.'

The beetle steered them back through the twisting network of tunnels, passing through eleven more vaults, before nudging the transport capsule towards a solid wall that rose up before them, as unforgiving as a cliff face.

Yaz didn't disguise her alarm. 'Uh, what is it doing?'

'It's perfectly safe,' the Doctor reassured her. 'I memorised the layout. That's not a solid wall, just a mirage.'

'Okay.' Yaz relaxed, but only for an instant as the Doctor went on.

'However, it's almost certainly a holographic shield wall. The wrong approach path – even by a millimetre – and *ka-blammo*! The trick to passing through one of these things safely is to hit it at just the right angle and velocity.'

'Don't say "hit it",' Yaz pleaded.

The nose of the transport capsule reared up, as the beetle wrenched the controls to one side then poured on the power. Suddenly they were upside down. Yaz felt her last meal make a dash for the exit, but the manoeuvre didn't seem to affect the Doctor at all.

'Killer bit of flying,' she said admiringly. 'A barrel roll. The Red Baron taught me how to do one. Not as easy as it looks.'

Still upside down, the transport capsule dived towards the wall. At the very last second, as the extremely solid-looking obstruction filled her vision, Yaz squeezed her eyes shut and braced for impact.

None came.

When Yaz opened her eyes again, she could see nothing for a moment but shapes in the darkness. Then, long-dormant bioluminescent lighting flickered into life at the arrival of the visitors.

The thirteenth vault lay before them.

The beetle set the transport capsule down next to a small pool. By the time Yaz had collected herself following the roller-coaster ride, the Doctor and the telepathic insect had already exited the capsule and she had to hurry after them.

This vault was half the size of the others, a forgotten cave lined not with towering pillars but with grey trees sculpted from solid rock. From unbending branches hung clusters of the same glass spheres she'd seen elsewhere. The cave looked like it should have been dank and musty, but a mysterious breeze moved the orbs in the trees, causing them to clink against one another like wind chimes.

'The Curatrix governs everything you have seen, except for this one chamber,' said the beetle. 'It cannot exist here. I am the Attendant, and the thirteenth vault is my domain. I am as much a part of this place as the rocks and earth.'

'You guard the thirteenth vault?' asked Yaz.

'I tend it. This vault contains the most highly prized seeds in the Galactic Seed Vault's collection.' It scuttled over to the nearest tree. 'Take this doppelpod from the planet Aether. Able to protect itself by mimicking the form of any predator that breathes on it. Or this Venusian gulper.' With a segmented limb, it indicated an orb above Yaz. 'Once the germination process begins, it is merely a matter of minutes before the plant achieves full growth. Remarkable life form.'

Yaz was struck by the Attendant's enthusiasm. She peered up at the orb containing the Venusian gulper, fascinated.

The Doctor snapped her fingers. 'That's the one that consumes its prey whole and digests it over a period of several months, right?'

Yaz backed away from the orb quickly.

The Attendant made a sound halfway between a hiss and a sigh. 'It is true that some unenlightened creatures would call the contents of this vault . . . dangerous.' Its tone altered. 'But there exists just one seed in the universe that truly deserves that description.'

The beetle turned its head to gaze across the pool. There, set into a flat section of rock, was a small wooden door.

What could possibly be worse than that Venusian gulper? Yaz wondered.

The Doctor skirted the pool to stand in front of the door, then studied it in silence. It was constructed from stout oak planks, darkened with age, their surface filled with black metal studs. The door was surrounded by a stone arch, and two large leaf-shaped hinges secured it to the frame. There was no visible lock, only a sturdy metal ring at waist height.

The Doctor reached out, but as her hand neared the ring it slowed, as if it was suddenly moving through water. No matter how long she persisted, she just couldn't seem to get her hand any closer.

She glanced at the pool.

Yaz followed her gaze, and for the first time noticed the ripples in the water. They were still, as if someone had dropped a pebble in the centre of the pool and then time itself had stopped.

The Doctor's eyes widened minutely, and she began to babble. 'So that's what the Time Lords were doing here. It's one of Zeno's paralocks.'

As usual, Yaz felt herself playing catch-up. 'Doctor, who is –'

'Zeno was a Time Lord who hypothesised one of the most secure locking mechanisms in the universe. It was rumoured that he built three examples – the paralocks – but I've never come across any of them. Until now.' She paused, contemplating the door. 'You see, between us and this door lies the most impenetrable substance imaginable: time. Years of the stuff. *Aeons*. You could try for as long as you liked to grasp that handle, but you'd never close the gap.' She joggled her head, revising her statement. 'Well, technically speaking, you would eventually get there, but you'd have to stand here for about sixteen billion years.'

'What's inside there that needs to be protected behind all that time?' asked Yaz.

'The first seed in the collection,' said the Attendant. 'The most terrifyingly beautiful thing you will ever behold.'

'And why would we be beholding it?' said the Doctor.

'Because the noughtweed that has ravaged the other vaults is coming here.'

'But it won't get in,' said Yaz. 'Not for sixteen billion years, you said.'

'I'm afraid it won't take that long,' said the Doctor. 'The problem with Zeno's paralocks is that they aren't as impenetrable as he theorised. Remember that diagram of the noughtweed's structure that the Curatrix showed us? It showed that the Gardeners had modified the plant with a time propagator. Once that weed's at the door, I estimate it will cut through the paralock in fewer than forty-eight hours.'

'But can't we stop it?' said Yaz. 'I mean, if it's a weed, isn't there some kind of intergalactic weedkiller we can spray on it?'

The Attendant's mandibles wobbled, which Yaz took to be the equivalent of shaking its head. 'The Curatrix was right. You cannot save the Galactic Seed Vault. Its destruction is inevitable. But, when the seed vault falls, what lies behind this door must be gone from here. If not, the consequences will be apocalyptic.'

'And why, exactly?' the Doctor asked.

The Attendant clicked softly, its mandibles fluttering. 'The universe is a garden that has been growing for tens of billions of years and, like everything that grows, one day it will wither and die. When that time comes, it is said that the First Gardener will return to re-seed the darkness with life, using the single seed that she locked behind this door. She named it the Genesis Seed. The one you know as Nightshade believes that now is the time for the universe to be renewed, that "the soil must be turned". If he secures the Genesis Seed before we do . . .' The beetle's voice trailed off, as if it was too horrified to finish. It paused before continuing. 'The Genesis Seed was never meant to be used on an inhabited universe. You, Doctor, must remove the seed to a safe place – or all life will be wiped out.'

Yaz reeled at the Attendant's words. It was asking them to prevent the end of the universe. The responsibility was incomprehensible. She studied the Doctor for her reaction. Presented with a mission of such magnitude, most people would resist the call, others would point-blank refuse, and the rest would at least question their role. But the Doctor wasn't other people, and Yaz knew that she had already accepted the task. Even in a universe clouded with uncertainty, the Doctor seemed to always instinctively know the right thing to do. Sure, that usually involved hurling herself and her companions into unfathomable danger, but that kind of went with the territory.

'So how do we get in then?' asked Yaz.

'A key,' said the Doctor. 'The right key will pass straight through the time barrier and fit the lock.' She peered closely at the door. 'Where is the lock?'

'It will appear when you have all the keys,' said the Attendant. 'There are three.'

'Aha. And I'm guessing they're not hanging on one of those little hooks on your kitchen dresser? No!' She suddenly slapped her head. 'Of course! Where is the dresser? That is the question. Somewhere far, far away from this door, naturally. Do you follow?'

'Um, not really,' said Yaz.

The Doctor sighed impatiently. 'The Time Lords who helped the First Gardener didn't just instal the paralock. They also scattered the keys throughout space and time.'

The Attendant nodded. 'In order to open the door, all three keys must be retrieved and turned simultaneously.'

'Oh, this is brilliant.' The Doctor clapped her hands together gleefully. 'I haven't had to collect a set of apocalypse-averting keys for *ages*. Three should be simple enough. Last time it was one, but in six pieces.' She struck off towards the transport capsule. 'Well, what are we waiting for? When the noughtweed reaches this vault, we'll only have forty-eight hours left to find those keys and get back here. I've always found that earth hours are the best for countdowns. Those final seconds make a lovely ticking sound.'

They rounded the pool, but hadn't gone far when there was a movement in the shield wall. It shimmered, as a second transport capsule glided through and circled the vault.

'Who's that?' asked Yaz.

'I don't know,' said the Doctor. 'But something tells me they aren't here to deliver pizza.'

The capsule touched down in the centre of the vault, in a small clearing among the stone trees. The side hatch opened, and two familiar figures climbed out.

'Ryan! Graham!' Yaz ran delightedly towards them, then stopped. They were not alone.

From behind them strode three armoured Gardeners. Soldiers, judging by their appearance. Well, foot soldiers compared with the fourth figure who swaggered out of the capsule, and paused to survey the vault. He carried himself with a high-and-mighty air, as if years ago his dad had taken him aside, looked out over the world and said, 'One day, son, all this will be yours,' and today was that day.

There was no doubt in Yaz's mind. This was Deadly Nightshade.

'You two okay?' she called out.

'He took my car without asking and pranged it at McDonald's,' replied Graham.

'Seriously, get over it,' grumbled Ryan.

Yaz smiled, relieved to hear them arguing. 'Not sure you should be admitting to vehicular theft in front of a police officer.'

Nightshade adjusted his gloves, fitting them to his fingers before reaching into a holster and producing a stubby weapon. 'Kill them,' he commanded.

'Gotta respect that in a villain,' said the Doctor, pulling Yaz and the Attendant behind one of the stone trees and out of the firing line. 'No chat, just straight down to business.'

There was a whip crack, and the Gardeners' weapons shot out lengths of sticky vines. They flew across the vault, landing short of their targets. They lay still for a moment, then slithered towards the tree sheltering the three of them. One vine wrapped itself round Yaz's ankle, then writhed up her body to coil round her neck. To her horror, it began to squeeze.

Meanwhile, the Doctor and the Attendant were similarly tied up. The Doctor was wrestling with the bulging vine pressed to her throat, while the stricken beetle attempted to use its claws to snip its way free.

Yaz felt the vine's grip tighten on her throat. Any second now, she'd black out and that would be the end. She flung herself at the stone tree, hitting it with enough force to shake the branches. Two seed jars fell to the ground, and one shattered, exposing the seed within to the cold air. Gasping now, Yaz reached inside her coat and felt for the solid form of the thermos flask. With trembling fingers, she unscrewed the lid and upended the contents over the fallen seed.

The effect was instant. It was like watching a time-lapse from a nature documentary. Before her eyes, the seed germinated in seconds, sprouted, then grew into a fully fledged plant. Within a spiral of tough green leaves pulsed a flower like a fat red tongue edged with dozens of needles, the gleaming points oozing with sap. It was the plant the Attendant had pointed out earlier: the Venusian gulper.

Yaz grasped one end of the vine that was choking her, and shoved it at the gulper's licking tongue. Sensing the presence of food, the plant sunk a row of needles into the vine. Yaz immediately felt its grip slacken. The gulper's red tongue darted out, and with a great sucking noise it consumed the vine like a strand of spaghetti.

Yaz took a deep breath of the cold vault air, then raced to help the others. The Attendant had already chopped its attacker into pieces, which twitched on the ground for a second or two before withering into ashes. The Doctor, however, was staggering about, hands tearing at the tenacious shoot choking her. Yaz manoeuvred her towards the still-hungry gulper, and it immediately sucked down the hapless vine.

The Doctor studied the gulper warily. 'Back away. It should be about ready for another growth spurt.'

'You mean it isn't fully grown?'

No sooner had Yaz asked the question than the gulper's stem erupted like a magic beanstalk. Within seconds, the plant had reached the height of the stone trees, sprouting leaves and more tongue-like flowers as it grew. Hungry to feed its rapid growth, the pulsing tongues searched for food.

'Time we got going,' said the Doctor, pushing Yaz ahead of her towards the transport capsule.

The gulper's flowers greedily probed the air, turning slowly to face Graham, Ryan and the Gardeners. Hoisting itself up on a ball of writing roots, the plant skittered across the vault towards them. Two of the Gardener soldiers lay down covering fire, while Nightshade and the other soldier retreated up the ramp to the safety of their transport capsule.

Under cover of the commotion, Ryan and Graham ran to join Yaz and the Doctor.

'Quickly!' shouted the Attendant, beckoning to them from the other transport capsule.

The Doctor and her companions clambered aboard, and they blasted towards the shield wall. Just before they passed through it, Yaz glanced back to see the Gardeners fending off the gulper. On one hand she felt bad about unleashing it on them – but on the other they *had* tried to strangle her.

The transport capsule hurtled back through the individual vaults towards the main entrance. The noughtweed had spread. Yaz counted seven vaults now infected, their walls crumbling, seed jars lying in glass splinters on the floor.

As the Attendant brought them in to land at the transit station where they had first boarded, it indicated a small wooden box resting on the capsule's controls. 'Open it,' it instructed the Doctor.

She lifted the lid to find a single bluebell flower inside.

'The location of the three keys hidden by the Time Lords is encoded in this flower. Your timeship will be able to read the information.'

The Doctor picked the bluebell up carefully by the stem. The flower was the same shade as the TARDIS.

An alert sounded from the capsule's control panel, and the communication screen lit up with an incoming message. Nightshade. He and the other Gardeners, it appeared, had made it out in their capsule, though it looked as if one of them had lost an arm to the ravenous gulper. A centipede squirmed out of Nightshade's nose and across one cheek as he spoke. 'The thirteenth vault will fall, Doctor. The Genesis Seed will be mine. These things are as inevitable as autumn turning to winter.'

'On Dracorus 805-U, they only have one season,' said the Doctor. 'So, you see, what's inevitable for you isn't necessarily so for the rest of the galaxy.'

'All leaves will fall,' intoned Nightshade. 'The soil must be turned.'

With that he cut the communication, and the screen went dark.

9. The Last Guardians

The Doctor popped the navigational bluebell in one of the many interfaces on the TARDIS's console. 'There, the TARDIS should be able to read the information.'

'I still don't understand why we're rushing about looking for magical keys,' said Graham. 'We've got a time machine, right? So, why not just travel back in time to the Galactic Seed Vault *before* the germinator and his pals got in there and wrecked the place? We could stop all this before it even began. Begins?'

The Doctor nodded. 'Grammar – the first casualty of time travel.' She stepped round the console. 'But you make a good point.'

'I do?' Graham didn't hide his surprise.

'Of course, you're not right, but don't let that take the shine off.' She held up three fingers. 'There are three reasons why we can't fix the problem as you suggest. One: the possibility of generating a time paradox. We're already active in this timestream, so going back in time like that would run the risk we'd bump into different versions of ourselves. And, trust me, you don't want to meet yourself. Especially not you, Graham. Two: there are fixed points in time which cannot be altered. I suspect that the death of the Galactic Seed Vault is one of those points.'

She turned back to the console and began flipping switches.

'That's only two,' said Graham. 'What's the third reason?'

The Doctor minutely adjusted a dial, peered at it, then stepped back, apparently satisfied. 'Going back in time and preventing almost certain catastrophe with ages to spare?' She raised her eyebrows. 'Where's the fun in that?'

With a final flourish, she set the TARDIS in motion.

'Okay, let's find out where we're going.'

The blue box vanished, its wake kicking up a whirlwind of snow that showered the watching

Attendant. The beetle looked out at the white plateau it now stood on. It hadn't been outside for longer than it could remember, and it was old now – a great deal older than its shiny carapace would suggest. It shook off the coating of snow and turned back to the skiff that had brought them out here.

The skiff hadn't been used for millennia, but everything about the Galactic Seed Vault had been built – or, more accurately, grown – to last. It had started without a murmur, whisking them effortlessly from the transit station and out across the snowy wastes. Like the vault itself, the technology was reliable beyond the measure of most civilisations.

The Attendant's gaze settled on the angular shape at the foot of the now-distant mountains. Its duties lay back there, protecting the secret in Vault Thirteen – perhaps the greatest secret in the universe. Such a responsibility, and the source of endless bad dreams. It shivered, and not from the cold.

The Curatrix was waiting inside the skiff's cabin. The AI's presence wasn't limited to the vault, so long as there was some kind of carrier for its brain – in this case, the vessel's systems. It projected its glowering humanoid presence, clipboard in hand, tapping its foot in irritation.

The Attendant held up a foreleg to stall what it knew the Curatrix was about to say. It wasn't a gesture typical of its species, but it had seen the humans do something similar. It didn't help.

'You stridulating, compound-swivel-eyed *liar*.' Evidently the Curatrix had been waiting for the visitors to leave to lay into its colleague. 'Ten million years we've been together, and only today do I find out about Vault Thirteen?'

The beetle rubbed a hind leg nervously against its side. There was no point in mounting a defence. The Curatrix was right. Yes, the Attendant had only been following orders laid down by the vault's original creators, but that didn't change the fact of the deception. While it let the Curatrix pour out its vitriol, it sat in the pilot's seat, fired up the skiff's engines and lifted off, swinging the nose of the craft round to point back towards the Galactic Seed Vault.

As they sped across the snow, the Attendant considered the past and the future. The vault had always been protected by one Attendant and one Curatrix. The two of them were only the latest in a long line, mere youngsters in comparison with the age of the vault itself. The Attendant watched its fiery companion sadly. They would, it now appeared, be the last.

10. Dorm

The midday sun glared off the curved surface of the city of Dorm's protective dome. Outside the sealed environment of the city, the pitted surface of New Phaeton stretched for thousands of miles in every direction, dry as dust and nearly devoid of life.

In the central control room of Dorm's science department, one of the operators cycled the lock at the southern gate. The heat crackled at the widening gap, and out swarmed a squadron of tiny quadcopter drones. As they emerged from the shadow of the dome, on-board cameras began to stream video.

Back in the control room, the two operators watched the video feed on a bank of monitors, as they did every day, on high alert for intruders. Aaron (student number 357) observed his junior colleague Lalitha (student number 428). It was her first term in the control room, and she displayed the typical eager-to-please attitude that he recalled once possessing. He was older by two years, but his authority was undermined by what others referred to as his 'baby face'. The others didn't take him seriously, always assuming he was a lower year than he was. This was Aaron's last term, and tomorrow he would graduate with the rest of his cohort. The first graduation in the school's history, it was a big step into the outside world. By the end of it, they would all be dead.

One of the drones stopped broadcasting and its slaved monitor went dark. Aaron punched a few buttons, trying to determine what had gone wrong. He assumed from experience that it had either flown into a dust storm or, more likely, simply malfunctioned. Like the rest of the equipment in Dorm, the drones were held together with string and prayers. With no access to replacement parts or new kit, it was a constant battle to keep them flight-ready.

With a spark, another drone's monitor shorted out. At the same time, the screen next to it showed activity on the horizon.

'What's that?' asked Lalitha.

The drones were programmed to detect movement and home in on it. One of them had locked on to a target and was tracking its progress. Aaron sharpened the camera's focus. The target appeared to be a small, spinning blue box with a flashing light on the topside of its hull.

'Is it a Spectre?' asked Lalitha.

Aaron shook his head. 'Not like any I've seen before.' He plotted the box's current course. 'If it continues on this trajectory, it's going to crash against our shield.'

'There's nothing we can do,' said Lalitha. 'We can't lower it.'

Aaron knew she was right. To lower the defensive shield would go against everything they'd been taught since their first year of school. It was drilled into every child in the colony: keep the shields up and the Spectres out. But in that moment something possessed him. A wild impulse to break the rules. Maybe the blue box was a rescue ship? Maybe the outside world hadn't forgotten about them, after all?

For years, he had been taught to trust only the Faculty. Now, though, he decided to trust himself.

He lowered the south shield.

'Aaron! Are you mad?'

Ignoring Lalitha's objections, he watched as the blue box maintained its approach. It would reach safety in less than ten seconds, then he could re-energise the shields.

Another monitor caught his eye. To an inexperienced operator the image it displayed would have appeared to be nothing more than the shimmer of heat haze.

'Spectres inbound,' said Lalitha, who'd recognised the threat at the same time as Aaron. 'Quadrant four.'

Spectres. They were always out there, but not even a practised controller like Aaron could predict when they'd attack. The planet's native life forms, they were not consciously hostile to the inhabitants of Dorm; much like the earth's predatory sharks that children were taught about at school, the Spectres were only doing what came naturally. In the flesh, they looked more like jellyfish than sharks. Atop gelatinous bodies with trailing tentacles, their bell-shaped heads pulsed with light, each flash illuminating rows of needle-like teeth.

The incoming Spectres swarmed towards the gap in the protective dome. Aaron silently gave thanks that he couldn't hear their shrill and rasping voices. On his first day in the control room, he had accidentally left the drones' audio switched on, and the terrible noise still invaded his dreams.

'You have to raise the shield,' Lalitha urged.

He had to time it just right. If he reactivated the shield too soon, the blue box would smash against the electromagnetic barrier and in all likelihood be destroyed. Too late, and the Spectres would gain entry to Dorm.

He counted down in his head.

Three, two, one . . .

'Textbook landing,' said the Doctor, patting the console. 'Not that I've read it.'

Plan A had been to materialise inside the city, but the TARDIS's navigation systems had proved characteristically erratic, forcing the Doctor to make a more conventional approach through the planet's atmosphere. That had been Plan B. It could've been worse. Usually, they were lucky if they reached the heady heights of Plan F.

'So, where are we?' asked Ryan.

'Third planet in the Librae system,' said the Doctor. 'Its inhabitants call it New Phaeton.

Gravity is point nine of earth's, and the planet is home to a colony who've been here for a little less than ten years.'

'What about the key?' asked Graham.

'If you're expecting a big arrow with a sign that reads "Impossible Key This Way", you're going to be disappointed. We'll have to search for it.'

She consulted the external sensors, double-checked the atmosphere and, having confirmed that it was safe to breathe, opened the door. The TARDIS had landed close to a wall.

'This thing should come with sensors,' said Ryan.

'It does,' said the Doctor. 'Long range, short range, pan-dimensional.'

'Yeah, but not *parking* sensors,' he said, squeezing through the narrow gap.

They were in some kind of control room, and it was in chaos. An alarm wailed, and the hot smell of fused wires was overpowering. Smoke drifted from an open panel at which a young woman was directing a fire extinguisher. A baby-faced young man sat at a bank of monitors, desperately slapping buttons and spinning dials. They both wore threadbare survival suits that looked like they'd once been white but had faded to an indeterminate grey. The suits' rubber seals had perished long ago. They looked like they had been through a dozen owners.

Curiously, at their necks, the young woman and man both sported striped blue-and-white ties. Neither seemed to have noticed the TARDIS – or, if they had, they were too embroiled in their urgent tasks to pay it or the new arrivals any attention.

'We're fifteen seconds from a breach,' the young man shouted over the din.

The Doctor didn't wait to be invited to help. 'Your shield – is the technology gravity-based or electromagnetic?'

He whirled round, his eyes wide with surprise. 'Who are –'

'Which one?' she demanded.

'Electromagnetic,' he blurted.

The Doctor whipped out her sonic screwdriver, made an adjustment and then, scrutinising the equipment, found the section she wanted and plunged in. The sonic fired. 'This will temporarily boost the signal.'

There was a brief pause, then the young man watched the power-management readout on his display tick upwards. 'It's working,' he muttered in amazement.

On the monitors, the protective dome sparked repeatedly as Spectres slammed against it. With each collision, the shimmering beings dispersed in a flash of heat and light.

'Thank you,' he mumbled.

'I have a feeling I should be thanking you, . . .'

'Aaron,' he said, completing the Doctor's sentence. 'And this is Lalitha.' He gestured at the young woman, who was still holding the fire extinguisher and scowling at him.

'Well, Aaron, first off, commiserations on having parents who couldn't be bothered making it past page one of *The Big Book of Baby Names*. Second, and more importantly, according to the settings on these controls, someone lowered the shield to let us through safely.' She smiled her thanks and pocketed the sonic. 'Also, your generator core needs a service. One big hit and the whole thing will collapse. I can take a look at it, if you'd like. Oh, and have you seen a key?' She spread her thumb and forefinger apart. 'About yay big. Opens a secret vault from the beginning of time.'

'Uh . . .'

'No rush. Have a think.'

'What were those things trying to get in?' asked Yaz.

'We call them Spectres,' explained Aaron, clearly still reeling from their sudden arrival.

He stared past them in wonder at the TARDIS. 'How did you –'

'Some kind of energy-based life form,' the Doctor said to Yaz, cutting Aaron off. 'Judging by their interaction with the protective shield out there.'

Aaron nodded. 'They drain the life force of whatever they come into contact with.'

'Space vampires,' mumbled Ryan.

'They try to enter Dorm, and we keep them out. It's been this way since the first intake.'

'Be careful,' warned Lalitha, her eyes darting to a camera nestled high in one corner of the room. 'You shouldn't be talking about such things without permission.'

'Doc,' Graham called. 'Take a look at this.'

On the wall next to the TARDIS, half obscured by it, was a sign in English that read: SS *PHAETON* – DECK 12.

Graham frowned. 'This is some kind of ship.'

'The *Phaeton* left earth in the year 4018,' Aaron said. Something about these visitors – and especially the woman who had fixed the shield – gave him the confidence to speak freely.

Yaz couldn't hide her surprise. 'This is an earth ship?'

Aaron nodded. 'We were heading for the Avolantis System, but encountered a solar storm and crashed here. Ever since then we've been trying to contact earth. It's been ten years.'

The Doctor frowned. 'But there was no distress signal. The TARDIS would have noticed.'

'That's impossible,' blurted Lalitha.

'Trust me,' the Doctor said. 'There isn't a single man-made radio wave coming off this planet. You're not so far from some of the main space shipping lanes, but a vessel could pass within a thousand miles of your atmosphere and not know anyone was down here.'

'But that can't be.' Aaron looked confused. 'Why would the Faculty lie?'

Yaz offered a consoling smile. 'People in charge sometimes fudge the truth when the situation is too terrible.'

'Don't worry,' said Graham. 'We can get you off this rock. I could fit sixty kids on an old Wrightbus, and the TARDIS can take a lot more than that. How many of you are there?'

'The roll stands at a little over five hundred students,' said Aaron.

'And adults?' said the Doctor.

'Not a single adult survived the crash,' said Aaron.

'You mean apart from the Faculty?' said the Doctor.

Lalitha and Aaron exchanged looks. 'The Faculty is not like you,' he said.

They were interrupted by the sound of a musical chime, then a soothing voice issued from a public-address system.

'Infraction detected.' The tone was even. 'Student number 357, prepare for punishment.'

Lalitha looked at Aaron in horror. 'Oh, no.'

Aaron stiffened, bracing himself. As the others watched, his blue-and-white tie moved like a snake coiling in the grass. It tightened round his neck, the knot pressing against his throat and choking him, but he made no attempt to pull it off.

The Doctor leaped forward, sonic outstretched.

'No!' yelled Lalitha. 'If you interfere, it will kill him.'

After a few more seconds, the tie slackened and Aaron sank to his knees, gasping for air.

There was another series of musical chimes. 'Punishment concluded. Thank you for your co-operation. The Faculty – making your child's world better.'

While Yaz and Graham made sure Aaron was okay, the Doctor turned to Lalitha, her normally bright eyes blazing with anger. 'I'd like a word with your Faculty.'

Graham glanced at the Doctor. Their mission had been simple enough: collect the first key to the paralock. But, as with most things the Doctor dipped a toe into, the situation had already become complicated. Graham knew that, even if the key was presented to her now in a velvet-lined box, she wouldn't contemplate leaving – not after seeing that poor kid half strangled by his weird tie. Whatever the truth was behind this starship school, it was clearly a bad place, and these kids were in danger from the Spectres outside. Graham knew they weren't leaving this planet until the Doctor ensured that every last child was safe.

Lalitha glanced at a monitor which showed a handful of young men and women marching along a corridor. 'Perfects.'

Ryan looked puzzled. 'You mean prefects, right?'

The control-room door slid open, and the group trooped inside, their backs as rigid as their formation. The Perfects were dressed like Aaron and Lalitha, but their survival suits boasted shield-shaped badges decorated with a curling letter P set against an insignia of a sunburst and a chariot. Their leader, in his late teens with a thin face and a faint fuzz of moustache, brandished a device: a small box with two electrodes between which an electrical spark sizzled. It looked like some kind of taser.

'Porter,' Aaron said to the leader. 'You don't need that. They're here to help.'

Porter studied the Doctor and her companions in silence, at once fascinated by and fearful of the new arrivals. Finally, he stepped forward and raised the taser.

'Take them to detention.'

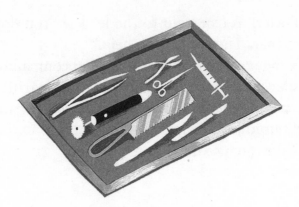

11. Please, Miss,
I Feel Sick

The hatch in the cell door banged shut, and the click of the Perfects' footsteps receded along the corridor.

'Seventeen minutes,' announced the Doctor. 'Between landing and being arrested. A new record.' She grinned.

Graham shook his head. The Doctor had some funny ideas.

The Perfects had led them from the control room along the crumbling passageways of the crashed starship to their present location. They'd had to pick their way across fallen beams, navigate tangles of bent and twisted metal, and skirt around open wall panels from which spilled nests of fused wires. The place was a wreck. From what Graham could establish of the layout, the vast ship formed the central structure of what the inhabitants called the city of Dorm. At some point since their crash landing, a dome shield had been added, like a protective umbrella, enclosing the ship from nose to tail. Everyone they'd passed had walked by in perfect silence, and they all wore one of those strangling ties. Pacifying technology, the Doctor had called it, to keep them in line.

When they reached the detention level, Graham and the Doctor had been separated from Yaz and Ryan. The Doctor also had her sonic confiscated, so there'd be no easy escape this time. They were then led through a cold and cavernous room filled with ranks of what at first looked to Graham like coffins. When they passed the first one, he was shocked to find the upper half of the lid was transparent, revealing the occupant. He paused next to it. Inside was a child no more than eight years old. Alongside was a humming monitor, which displayed information like heart rate and oxygen levels.

'Hibernation pods,' explained the Doctor, as they walked. 'The passengers sleep away long journeys between the stars.'

They passed many more pods like the first, and each one contained a young man or woman. Graham stopped counting at fifty.

'Why aren't they awake like everyone else?' he asked Porter, the Head Boy.

'This is the new intake.' He threw a fearful glance over his shoulder, as if worried he'd get into trouble for talking to them. 'There are hundreds more pods throughout the ship. When we graduate, the Faculty will wake the next lot.' He stroked his tie nervously.

'And how does that work, the old school tie?' asked the Doctor.

Porter lowered his voice. 'The Faculty has a keypad implanted in one palm. Every student has a number, so all it has to do is input the relevant number. Classes have numbers too, so it can punish individual students or the entire school.'

Taking great care, the Doctor grasped one edge of Porter's tie and flipped it over. There was a label underneath with space for his name, which was handwritten in red ink, and a flashy logo featuring what looked like a robotic fist against a star field.

'Paragon Teletronics of Sirius,' she said, recognising the logo, then fell silent.

Graham could tell that she was figuring something out. He hoped it was a way out of this nightmare.

Leaving the hibernation chamber, they passed into a hallway lined with hulking metal-framed doors complete with food hatches and magnetic locking mechanisms. Prison doors. Here, he and the Doctor were deposited in a cell that looked like a converted classroom. A shaft of afternoon light shone down through a sliver of window, picking out a young woman about eighteen years old who was sitting at a school desk, writing in a notebook. Like the other students, she wore a battered survival suit and tie.

Looking up from her work, she stared at the Doctor and Graham through the milk-bottle lenses of a pair of thick-rimmed spectacles. 'Who are you?' she asked.

'I'm the Doctor, and this is Graham. What's your name?'

'Peyton, but everyone calls me Moley.' She peered at Graham. 'You're so . . . lined.'

'Charming,' said Graham. 'No wonder she's in jail.'

'I'm sorry.' Peyton's voice dropped. 'It's been a long time since I saw anyone like you. Not since my father sent me away . . .'

Graham felt bad for poking fun at the girl. 'So, what you in for?' he asked. 'Last time I was in detention it was for blowing spitballs at Nancy Green in Mr Tanner's maths class.'

'That's disgusting,' said the Doctor, curling her lip. She turned to Peyton. 'Mol– no. Can't do it, sorry. Peyton, you said your father sent you away?'

She nodded. 'I was part of the first intake.'

The Doctor looked up, her eyes bright with understanding. 'I think I know what this place is. The *Phaeton* was carrying a boarding colony.'

'I don't understand,' said Graham.

'On earth in your time, some parents send their children away to boarding school, right? Well, that tradition continued into the forty-first century, but with population growth at an all-time high only the extremely rich were able to send their children to earth schools. Off-world boarding colonies were established for everyone else. From what Peyton here is saying, it appears that the SS *Phaeton* was travelling to one of them. When it crashed, the surviving students built a society based on the only thing they knew.'

'Boarding school,' said Graham, understanding.

'Now, if you will excuse me, I have to think.' The Doctor sat down on the floor, crossed her legs and closed her eyes in meditative silence.

Peyton's expression curled in confusion. 'What did she mean "in your time"? It was like she was giving you a history lesson.'

'She was. The Doc is a time traveller,' explained Graham. 'Been flying around the universe solving problems and saving lives for thirteen generations.'

Peyton's mouth gaped. 'A time traveller?' She looked at Graham. 'And you?'

'Yup. Well, time *hitch-hiker* might be more accurate. Though, if we're taking in the whole career path, I average out to bus driver.'

'A time-bus driver,' said Peyton in wonder.

'No, I – never mind.' He glanced at the Doctor, still sitting there in a bubble of calm contemplation. Who knew where her mind had drifted off to? To kill the time, he decided to tell Peyton about their mission, the Gardeners and the key to Vault Thirteen.

When he'd finished, the girl thought for a moment before speaking. 'Would this key open the door to a garden?'

'That would make sense,' said Graham. 'I mean, about as much sense as stashing three magical keys throughout time and space.'

'The Faculty carries a set of keys,' she said. 'One opens the door to Plainfield. It's the only place in Dorm where there are trees and flowers. It's not for ordinary students. Only Perfects like Porter are allowed in, and even then on just one day a year. I've seen pictures. It's beautiful. The Faculty spends most of its time there.'

'Typical,' said Graham. 'The teachers at my school had a staffroom like that. Rumour had it there was a tropical aquarium in there and unlimited Wagon Wheels.'

Graham felt as certain as he could that the key to Plainfield must also be one of the keys to Vault Thirteen. Not that the information was much use to him in here.

'So, where is this Plainfield then?' he asked.

'The only access is through the Head's study,' said Peyton. 'But you can't get in. The Faculty won't let you.'

'Don't worry, the Doc will find a way. It's kind of her thing. We just need to get out of here.'

'Well, it had better happen before tomorrow,' said Peyton dismally. 'It's graduation. The first in the school's history. That's why I'm in here. I tried to escape the ceremony.'

Graham looked confused. 'When I was your age, I was desperate to leave school and get out into the world.'

'Then our worlds must be very different.'

'She's right,' the Doctor piped up, opening one eye.

'Finished your Time Lord yoga, then?' said Graham.

'I'll have you know that I have been meditating on a plan to save the school. One that doesn't involve organising a dance.' She paused. 'And Time Lord yoga's on Thursdays.' She jumped to her feet. 'Notice that smell in the air?'

Graham sniffed. 'Damp PE kit?'

The Doctor sighed. 'Atmosphere scrubbers struggling to recycle what little air they've got in here. Beyond the protective habitat of the dome, this planet can't support human life. And, even if it could, the only things out there are the Spectres. Peyton's not in here because she has an aversion to wearing a gown and mortarboard.'

A horrified expression slid across Graham's face, as the fate of the graduates struck him a moment before the Doctor uttered the words aloud.

'She's in here because graduation means death.'

Just then, the hatch on the door opened and Porter's beady eyes and fuzzy moustache appeared in the gap. 'The Faculty will see you now.'

*

Ryan moved closer to the cell door and let out a loud, hacking cough.

'You okay?' asked Yaz.

'I'm fine,' he whispered. 'I'm trying to get us out of here. See, I pretend to be sick, they open up to investigate, and we seize the chance to escape. It's a classic move, trust me.' With that, he coughed again, this time clutching his stomach and throwing in a cry of pain for good measure.

Yaz shook her head. 'That's never going to work.'

The hatch in the cell door banged open. One of the Perfects studied Ryan.

'I think I'm going to be sick,' he moaned, writhing about.

The Perfect touched his shield badge, which apparently doubled as a communicator, and spoke into it. 'Possible biohazard in detention.'

'Yeah, that's it,' said Ryan, playing up to the diagnosis. 'I'm hazardous. You'd better get me out of here. Sharpish.'

The Perfect ignored him. 'Female prisoner has also been exposed.'

'I'm fine,' protested Yaz.

'No, you're not,' insisted Ryan.

The Perfect listened for a moment. 'Acknowledged. Bringing them to the San right away.'

Ryan shot Yaz a smile of victory. 'Told ya,' he whispered.

'Engaging infection protocol,' said the Perfect. He reached for the neck of his survival suit and released an integrated hood, which he pulled up to cover his head.

'Seems a bit extreme,' said Ryan, as a handful of hood-wearing Perfects arrived to escort them away.

They were led deeper into the ship, passing through ten deck levels of the enormous vessel, until they came to a brightly lit section with antiseptically white walls and floors. The Perfects suddenly dropped back, leaving a gap between them and their prisoners.

Ryan had been biding his time, hoping for an opportunity to make an escape. Now was the moment. He cast a knowing glance at Yaz, and they broke into a run. Risking a look over his shoulder, Ryan was puzzled to see that the Perfects were making no attempt to pursue them. If anything, they seemed unwilling to follow. Though it struck him as a bit strange, it made getting away a lot easier.

He and Yaz skidded round a corner and found themselves face to face with a door marked SANATORIUM. With no other option, they went through it.

Inside was a long, thin room that stretched so far into the distance the other end lay in shadow. The walls glowed with tiles whiter than a film star's teeth, and the floor had been polished to the sheen of a skating rink. There was so much bleach in the air it stung Ryan's eyes and throat.

Along one wall was a line of beds, crisp sheets stretched drum-skin tight over the mattresses. Next to each bed was a table, on which sat a bowl of grapes and a vase of flowers. Both the fruit and flowers had been there so long they had rotted away, and the sweet whiff of decay mixed in with the pervasive smell of cleaning products.

One of the beds was occupied.

'Hello,' Ryan called, his voice bouncing off the room's hard surfaces.

There was no answer, so he moved closer and, as he did, he saw that the bed's occupant had pulled the sheet up over their head. Gingerly, Ryan gripped the sheet's edge and drew it down.

As soon as he saw what was beneath the sheet, he hurriedly stepped away, tripping over his own feet. It wasn't a person in the bed. At least, not a living person. Staring back at him were the empty sockets of a human skull, a skeleton with bones as white as the polished tiles.

From the shadows at the far end of the room came a noise: the squeak of a wheel in need of oil. Ryan looked round. Out of the darkness trundled a robot, vaguely triangular in shape, its wheels hidden beneath the lower flared section. Its body was almost entirely white, but painted across its midsection was a red cross. Six spindly metal arms projected from the upper body, each ending in multi-segmented fingers clearly designed for delicate work. At the top of the triangle perched a smooth white oval that resembled a human head, but was featureless save for a pair of empty eye sockets. A surgical mask covered the lower half. Even though the eye sockets were empty, Ryan had the strong suspicion that the machine was watching him and Yaz.

It rolled to a stop in front of them. 'I am Automated Medical System Version Eight, but you may call me M8-Tron,' said a brusque female voice. 'You both require pink medicine.'

Two of its arms shot out, pinning both Ryan and Yaz by their throats.

Ryan attempted to break free, but M8-Tron's grip was too strong. He tried a different approach, attempting to protest that he felt fine actually, but all that came out was a gurgle. He could only watch as a drawer slid out of the robot's middle, and two more arms dipped into it then reappeared. One held a large brown bottle, the other a silver spoon. The robot carefully measured out a dose of gloopy pink liquid, then raised the spoon. There was the whir of actuators, and Ryan felt metal fingers prise his lips apart.

'Open wide.'

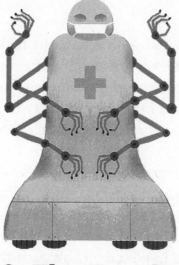

12. The Faculty

The Faculty occupied a section of the ship that looked like the interior of an old country house on earth. The walls were swathed in dark wood panelling, a dusty chandelier hung from the ceiling, and a creaking staircase curved up to the floor above.

The Doctor and Graham were waiting in a hall outside a door marked HEAD. On one side of the door was a glass cabinet filled with trophies and pennants, and on the other side a softly ticking grandfather clock. As Graham listened to it, he noticed a board with a list of names picked out in gold lettering on the wall opposite. Against each name was engraved the same date, and with a pang he realised it must be the date of the crash. The board was a memorial to those who had died. He barely had time to dwell on the sad history of this strange school when the Doctor snatched his attention away.

She was prowling around the grandfather clock, eyeing it suspiciously. When she had examined it from every angle, she pounced, wrenching the cabinet open like a magician whipping a handkerchief away at the climax of a grand illusion.

'Aha!'

Inside, the pendulum swung steadily.

The Doctor uttered a disappointed, 'Oh.'

'What were you expecting?' asked Graham.

She rapped the outside of the clock's case. 'Knew someone once who had a TARDIS that looked just like one of these.' She glanced around the hall. 'This is just his or her sort of twisted idea of fun.'

Graham was curious to learn more, but before he could enquire further a voice boomed from the other side of the door.

'Enter!'

He clenched his hands. His palms felt sweaty. Even after all these years, there was nothing like a teacher's command to instil fear and trepidation.

The Head's office was much like the hall. Portraits of grave-faced educators hung against the oppressive wood panelling. Some of the frames were singed, presumably damaged in the crash. Briefly, Graham wondered why anyone would have gone to the bother of transporting such dreary art all the way from earth.

There was a door against the back wall marked FACULTY ONLY. According to Peyton, that was the way into Plainfield. Next to it sat a wide desk, which was presently unoccupied, and on top lay what appeared to be a stack of brochures. The image on the cover showed a smiling pair of schoolchildren standing on what looked like the surface of Mars, waving at the camera while wearing what could only be described as school-uniform spacesuits. Along the bottom of the picture ran the slogan *Your child's future begins here!* It was a prospectus for the boarding colony.

The door marked FACULTY ONLY swung open, and into the study shambled a creature that was human – more or less. In the centre of its shoulders sat a male head, plump and saggy like a piece of fruit that had been left too long in the bowl. Next to it was a second head, this one female, with a thin and tight-lipped face and dark hair piled into a bun. From one side of its body extended an arm that was bare and brawny, with a rolled-up white shirtsleeve and a pale, hairy forearm. It wore a wristwatch with a large round dial. Meanwhile, on the other side was an arm clothed in chiffon that draped across a dark, skinny arm ending in a hand with long, tapering fingers dotted with bright red nail varnish. In the middle, beneath a section of tweed jacket, bulged the sort of chest you'd encounter on a classical statue during a school trip to a museum.

'Visitors!' exclaimed the male head, in the same booming voice Graham had winced at outside the room. There was no doubt in Graham's mind that he was the school's Head. 'We haven't had visitors in such a long time.'

The hairy arm shot out, indicating a couple of chairs.

'Please, take a seat,' said the female head.

The creature limped to the desk. One powerful leg wore half a pair of red tracksuit bottoms and a single white trainer; the other was encased in an opaque black stocking that slid into a black patent-leather high heel. The legs were different lengths, giving the creature its distinctive gait. It had apparently learned to cope quite well with the whole odd arrangement, and was surprisingly nimble on its mismatched feet.

At each shoulder and at the top of the tracksuit-clad leg, Graham could distinctly make out deep stitches of surgical thread wound into exposed flesh, as if the various body parts had been roughly sewn together. Aaron had said that not a single adult had survived when the SS *Phaeton* crashed. Clearly, what he meant was that not one *whole* adult survived. This creature wasn't simply wearing a patchwork of clothes; it was a collection of different teachers. A leg from PE, an arm from science, another from modern languages, a Head and a Deputy Head – all surgically joined together.

It was Frankenstein's monster's staffroom.

As the creature lowered itself into the chair behind the desk, a jangle sounded at its hip. With a thrill of excitement, Graham saw a collection of keys looped on to its belt. One of them had to be the key to Plainfield – and to Vault Thirteen.

'Welcome to Dorm,' beamed the Head, throwing its arms wide.

'We are the Faculty,' added the Deputy Head.

The inside of Ryan's mouth tasted like something had died in there – something furry and evil. The room swam before his eyes, and he couldn't feel his legs. It took him a moment to realise that he was lying in one of the beds, secured beneath its imprisoning bedsheet.

That vile pink medicine must have contained a sedative. He wasn't sure how long he'd been out of it, or what had happened to Yaz in the meantime. He tried to sit up, but the sheet pinned him like he was a plate of leftovers under a layer of cling film. With some effort, he twisted his neck to look across at the next bed.

Yaz lay there, completely still, her eyes closed. For a moment he had a terrible feeling that she was dead, but then to his relief she let out a loud snore.

He was distracted by a movement from across the room. His bleary eyes focused on M8-Tron fussing about next to a table. It was hard to tell exactly what the robot was up to, but then he caught the gleam of a blade under the bright lights and saw that it was cleaning a set of surgical instruments. As it went about its business, the robot hummed to itself.

'Yaz,' Ryan hissed.

One eyelid fluttered open, and Yaz squinted in the harsh overhead lights.

'We have to get out of here,' he whispered urgently. 'I think that weird robot is about to perform some kind of operation on us. And I'm guessing it's not the kind where you get ice cream afterwards.'

Yaz followed his gaze to the bustling robot and, recognising the imminent danger, began to wrestle with her own restraining bedsheet. Ryan renewed his struggle, squirming furiously in the hope of freeing himself.

M8-Tron, meanwhile, had apparently completed its preparations. The robot's triangular body pivoted round, and it squeaked across the shining floor towards their beds. In each of its six hands, it gripped a different surgical instrument: there were scissors, a grasper, spreaders, a needle, a scalpel and a rotating saw.

Ryan wrenched one shoulder against the sheet and finally felt a corner give. 'Yaz, we're getting out of here.'

'Silly boy,' cooed M8-Tron, closing in fast. 'No one leaves the Sanatorium.'

With a deep breath and a grunt of effort, Ryan tried again. This time, the bedsheet came loose. The robot loomed above him, a dark triangle against the lights. Three of its arms arced downwards. He saw the glint of multiple blades, and rolled sideways just in time to avoid the scalpel and needles that stabbed through the sheet where moments ago he had been lying. He tumbled out of bed and hit the floor, then quickly got to his feet. His legs felt like wet noodles.

'Ryan!' cried Yaz.

He side-stepped the robot's next attack, glimpsing the blur of its scything saw-arm and feeling it split the air next to his face. He spun round, grabbed the vase of rotting flowers on the bedside table, and hurled them into M8-Tron's face. A combination of desiccated daffodils and dirty water splashed into the robot's hollow eyes, and for a moment it was distracted.

A moment was all he needed. Ryan ripped off Yaz's sheet, yanked her out of bed, and together they bolted for the door.

The robot, having recovered from the assault, gave chase.

They sprinted back out of the Sanatorium, not sure where they were headed, but desperate to outpace the maniacal M8-Tron.

'Such naughty children.' Its irritatingly upbeat voice pursued them along the corridor.

Ryan tucked in behind the sprinting Yaz. She seemed to float, while he plodded. All his life he'd been rubbish at sports, but especially at school. He wasn't diagnosed with dyspraxia until he was in high school, and before that his clumsiness frequently made him the subject of cruel playground taunts. He couldn't kick a ball into an open goal to save his life, but what he lacked in co-ordination he made up for in determination.

'You keeping up?' shouted Yaz.

Ryan struggled to speak and run at the same time. 'Remember when you were at school,' he puffed. 'And everything came easy to you and your body never let you down embarrassingly in high-anxiety situations?'

'No.'

'Exactly.'

The passageway swept sharply to the left, and as they rounded the bend Ryan saw the doors to a lift.

'Stop at once!' yelled M8-Tron. 'That section is out of bounds!'

Ryan's heart was hammering in his chest, and he could hear the blood thrumming in his ears. Yaz glided towards the safety of the lift, while he still toiled in the runner-up position. Behind him, the squeak of M8-Tron's wobbly wheel grew louder. The robot was catching up.

Then he slipped on the polished floor. Losing his footing, he tumbled to the ground, striking his head. Dazed, he could hear Yaz shouting at him to get up, and he dumbly tried to obey. The lift doors were closing. He raised his head, but as he did so he felt the cold touch of M8-Tron's fingers. The robot looped a school tie briskly over him.

'Naughty, naughty,' it reprimanded. 'We don't want you to miss graduation.'

The tie tightened round Ryan's neck, and his world once again went dark.

13. Always Keep
the Warranty

'We're Mr and Mrs Smith,' said the Doctor. 'So lovely to meet you.' She extended her hand and clasped the Faculty's hairy hand, pumping it enthusiastically. Then she stepped back and, much to Graham's surprise, slipped an arm into his. 'We're checking out potential schools for our two little ones.' She jogged his arm. 'Isn't that right, darling?'

He'd been expecting the Doctor to roll out one of her big, confrontational speeches about protecting the universe from evil like the Faculty, and instead she had taken a slightly different approach. *Would've been helpful if she'd informed me first*, he thought, overcoming his initial confusion to play along.

'Uh, yeah, that is quite right.' His voice became gruff, as he tried to channel an old army man. 'My father went to a boarding colony, I went to a boarding colony, and so will my son and daughter.'

'Well, you couldn't choose a better school than New Phaeton,' said the Head, delightedly clapping one large hand against the other much smaller one. As it did so, Graham noticed a keypad embedded in the creature's palm. The keypad that Porter had said controlled the students' choking ties.

'Apologies for detaining you when you arrived.' The Deputy Head smiled. 'But one can never be too careful – and the children's welfare is our top priority.'

'Naturally,' agreed the Doctor.

'Just out of curiosity,' enquired the Head, turning to Graham. 'Where did you go to school, Mr Smith?'

'Mars,' he blurted. It was the first planet that came to mind.

'Home world of the Ice Warriors?' said the Deputy Head, and the Faculty raised all four eyebrows. 'I imagine that must have been quite a strict school.'

The Doctor shot Graham a look, then turned sweetly to the Faculty. 'How about a tour?' She detached herself from her fake husband, and headed towards the door in the back wall. 'Let's start in here. Have you got the key?'

The Faculty leaped to its feet and firmly guided her away from the door. 'I suggest we begin with the most important part of the tour. The heart of our school.' The two heads smiled in unison. 'The children.'

And so they trooped off along the corridor, listening to the Head and the Deputy Head take turns going on about the school's marvellous facilities, which included everything from a fully equipped zero-G gymnasium to anti-aircraft defences.

'Rassilon Junior and Sally,' the Doctor whispered to Graham.

'Hmm?'

'Our children's names. In case it should come up.' She gestured to the Faculty, currently several paces ahead of them and still boring on about the school. 'Rassilon Junior loves anything with wheels, though he's a cautious child, especially around roller coasters after an incident at Hedgewick's World of Wonders. And Sally is passionate about dinosaurs and climbing trees.'

'You've given this a lot of thought,' whispered Graham.

From up ahead came the sound of young voices raised in song. Graham could just make out the words.

'And did those boots in ancient time walk upon Phaeton's dusty land . . .' they trilled.

'Ah, the old school song,' said the Head, sweeping open a set of double doors.

Once, this had obviously been the ship's hangar bay, but now served as the school's assembly hall. A crumbling shuttle craft sagged at the edge of a yawning chamber, its parts long ago stripped to keep other, more important technology going.

Hundreds of children, organised by age, filled the space on two sides, leaving a corridor between them. The Faculty proceeded down this corridor with its familiar limping gait, heading towards a stage at the far end that was drawn with theatre curtains. As it passed the children, they sang out. Graham noted the fear in their eyes, as they shot sidelong glances at the terrible creature who ruled their lives.

The singers were accompanied by the *plink-plonk* of a badly played piano. Seated on the stage at an upright piano was a triangular white robot. Despite its six arms – or perhaps because of them – the sound it produced from the instrument was discordant and unsettling.

'Please,' said the Deputy Head, gesturing to two empty chairs right at the front of the hall. 'You'll be able to see everything from here.'

The Doctor and Graham took their seats, while the Faculty heaved itself up on to the stage and made its way to a speaker's dais set in front of the drawn curtains.

'Thank you, M8-Tron,' the Head said to the robot pianist, who ceased playing in a tumble of awkward notes.

There was a whine of feedback from the public-address system as the Head and the Deputy Head cleared their throats.

'Students, honoured guests, please join us in welcoming the class of 4028,' the Head declared with an expansive sweep of its modern-languages arm.

The curtains slid apart to reveal a row of seated students. Graham cast his gaze along the line, recognising among the blank faces Aaron, Peyton and Porter, the Head Boy – and, to his horror, right at the end of the row, Ryan.

'Take a long look, children,' the Deputy Head continued. 'Today we are here to say goodbye to them, for today they graduate.'

'I thought graduation was tomorrow,' said Graham in alarm.

'Our arrival has accelerated matters,' said the Doctor. 'Don't worry, it always does. Can't tell you how many invasions of earth have been brought forward because of me. I remember when a fleet of Dahensa warships suddenly appeared over London –' She caught Graham's eye. 'Probably not the moment.'

'No,' he confirmed.

The Doctor glanced towards the stage. 'Invaders are all the same, and the Faculty's no different. They don't want anyone spoiling their big day.'

A junior pupil approached, handing Graham and the Doctor each a sheet of paper. At the top of the page was written 'New Phaeton Graduation Day', and beneath it the running order for the service, including a list of hymns.

The Head boomed again. 'Now we shall sing hymn number one-three-eight, "How Deep the Faculty's Love for Us".'

There was the scrape of chairs on the floor as the school rose as one. Reluctantly, the students on stage followed the example of their younger counterparts. With a nod from the Deputy Head, the robot began to bash the piano once more, and the assembly hall filled with nervous singing.

The Faculty touched a control on the dais. There was a brief pause, then a grumble of machinery. Slowly, the wall behind the stage parted to expose the outside of the ship and the very edge of Dorm's protective dome. Built into the base of the dome was a large, round metal door – the outer seal of an airlock. Surveillance drones were regularly launched through this door into the wasteland beyond the ship, but for ten years no human had ventured outside. Until today.

A panel of lights turned from red to green, and with a pressurised hiss the internal airlock door swung open. Beyond lay a space the size of a large lift, ready for the graduates.

'Steeped in the disciplines of mathematics, Latin, physics and survival,' said the Head proudly, 'I estimate that the ablest students may live as long as three hours out in the world.' It applauded wildly, but no one else joined in.

Graham regarded the students seated on stage. For people facing certain death, they seemed remarkably calm. He peered into their faces, and the dull gleam in their eyes told him that they had been drugged into meek obedience – all of them but Ryan. He looked terrified.

145

The singing faltered, as a murmur of unease rippled through the hall. Some of the students at the front pointed. They'd spotted something beyond the dome.

Graham saw it too.

On the horizon was the distinctive shimmer of the Spectres. They were closing in on Dorm.

Yaz wandered the deserted passageways of the SS *Phaeton*, feeling guilty about leaving Ryan behind to the mercies of M8-Tron, but knowing that if she'd stayed to help she would have been captured too. She silently swore she'd find him *and* the key to Vault Thirteen. However, she couldn't deal with the medical robot on her own. She needed the others. The trouble was, they weren't on this deck.

There was also one other obstacle to her plan. She was lost.

The lift that had brought her to this level was somewhere far behind, in a maze of corridors that all looked the same. As yet, she hadn't come across another lift. All she knew was that this was deck thirteen, and that M8-Tron had yelled that it was out of bounds.

'I wonder why,' she muttered quietly to herself, as she reached another junction identical to all the others. 'Eeny, meeny, miny . . .'

The impact of the original crash had shattered the *Phaeton*'s interior, but some sections were more damaged than others. This one was the worst spot she'd encountered so far. Dust lay thickly on every surface, as if no one had visited this part of the ship in years. The ceiling had caved in at various points, peppering the route with debris. She stepped over a lump of twisted metal, and continued on down the passageway.

At the next junction, she found a directional sign on the wall, obscured by an accumulation of dirt. She rubbed away at it to reveal the words COMMUNICATION CENTRE.

A few minutes later, she found herself in a control room similar to the one where the TARDIS had set down. But, where that one had been filled with activity and the hum of power, here the monitoring positions were unmanned and the equipment silent. Nonetheless, she was at the very heart of the ship's communications systems. No wonder this place was out of bounds.

The students believed that, since the crash, the ship had been broadcasting an emergency distress signal, but the Faculty wouldn't want them to know that was a lie. For any normal teacher it would have been a priority: protect the children, send for help. But something had gone terribly wrong on New Phaeton.

Yaz could only imagine the horror that must have followed the crash. Whatever had happened must have driven the teachers and M8-Tron completely mad.

As Yaz tried to rid herself of the image, she wondered if perhaps she could get the equipment working and transmit an emergency distress signal herself. The lift, the lights – there was power on this deck, that much she knew. But how to bring the ship's communications back to life? The Doctor would have known which buttons to press, although Ryan had confided in her that the Doctor's approach to most technology seemed to be to press *all* the buttons.

She studied the control desk for a clue, circling it twice before she spotted a fat booklet propped between a couple of sliders. She picked it up, and turned to the first page.

Congratulations on purchasing the Nanospatial 5000, the latest in modular interstellar communications, from your friends at Paragon Teletronics.

It was the user manual.

The Nanospatial 5000 comes with a two-year universal warranty. Not valid on Mars.

She flicked to the contents page, and ran her eye down the headings: *Intro, Assembly, Software Installation, Quickstart . . .*

Okay, she thought, *let's give this a go.*

14. School's Out

The last lines of the third and final hymn of the ceremony tingled to the lofty ceiling of the assembly hall, and the students once more took their seats.

Ryan touched the tie round his throat. Past M8-Tron, he could see the Doctor and Graham in the audience, but what could they do? The Faculty held all the power, literally, in the palm of its hand. With one press of a key, it could cause agony – or worse – to every child in this room.

'So smart and well behaved,' said M8-Tron cheerily. Its musical duties performed, the robot passed along in front of the graduating class.

'You older students must set a good example to the younger ones. Now, a dose of pink medicine will help to dull the pain.' It began measuring out a spoonful for Ryan.

'I'm not in pain,' he said through gritted teeth.

M8-Tron's voice retained its unflinchingly cheery tone. 'Oh, but you will be.' The robot trundled closer. 'When the Spectres eat you alive.'

The Faculty stood at the dais, beaming from ear to ear to ear to ear, greeting the graduating students as they walked forward, shaking hands and passing out certificates. As each student collected their diploma and returned to his or her seat, there was a muted round of applause from the audience of schoolchildren. To Graham, it sounded like blasters firing. In just a few minutes, Ryan and the others would be flung out into the wasteland, at the mercy of the Spectres.

'Doc, we have to do something,' he urged.

'I already did,' she said, pulling herself out of her chair and leaping lightly on to the stage. She snatched a diploma meant for one of the graduates out of the Faculty's hands.

'This is most irregular,' said the Head. 'Please sit down, Mrs Smith.'

At the end of the row, Ryan frowned. 'Mrs Who?'

Even M8-Tron was distracted by the unusual development. Its brimming medicine spoon froze midway to Ryan's mouth.

The Doctor reached past the Faculty for the microphone. 'Paragon Teletronics,' she said, the words booming out across the assembly hall.

'Really, madam, this interruption will not do.'

She ignored the Head and carried on addressing the children. 'One of the most successful, innovative manufacturers of military and law-enforcement technology in this time period. Thing is, there was a scandal – or, I should say, there will be, about twenty years from now. It happens when users discover that the company included a secret line of code in all their products. See, Paragon wanted customers to buy their shiny new gyrovariable handcuffs or supersonic frosted riot shield or –' she turned to the nearest student, who happened to be Aaron, and tweaked his tie – 'vibrospatial strangulator. And, while many were happy to queue up for the latest version, most didn't bother upgrading until theirs broke. So Paragon decided to help that along, by including a kill code.'

Sensing danger, the Faculty raised the palm with the embedded keypad.

'I warn you,' said the Head, and the Deputy Head finished, 'one more word and I will severely punish the entire school.'

The Doctor barrelled on. 'The kill code lets you slow down the processor, drain the battery or even knock out the whole device.'

'That is quite enough!' bellowed the Head, tapping at the keypad. 'School, prepare for collective punishment.'

Graham turned to look out over the audience. The children winced in expectation, but when their terrible ties failed to stir their expressions changed to puzzlement.

'This is . . . can't be. Wait just one moment.' The Faculty stabbed furiously at the keypad.

'It won't help,' said the Doctor. 'Not even if you turn it off and on again.'

Graham could sense the mood in the hall alter. The cowed silence that had lain over the room like a cold fog began to lift. Whispered conversations broke out among the children. He heard excited snatches.

'It's not working!'

'Can't hurt us!'

All four eyes of the Head and Deputy Head blazing, threads of angry spittle at both of their mouths, the Faculty rounded on the Doctor. 'B-but how?' stuttered the Deputy Head.

The Doctor smiled. 'To trigger the kill code you just have to know the secret handshake.' She waggled a hand.

At last, the Faculty understood. The Head gazed in horror at the Doctor's extended hand. 'In the study . . . when you shook my . . .'

'Exactly.' She smiled, then became serious. 'Of course, it is possible to kill the kill code itself, if you remember to alter the default settings. But no one in the history of the universe has ever altered the default settings.'

There was panic in all four of the Faculty's eyes, then both mouths screamed, 'Noooo!'

'Doctor, look out!' Graham shouted.

M8-Tron was making its way across the stage at speed. Scalpels and surgical saws gleaming in several outstretched arms, the robot launched itself at the Doctor. 'I will not have such disobedience in my school. It's the Sanatorium for you, young lady.'

Ryan sprinted after the robot, and with a running jump he threw himself on to its back. 'Here, have a dose of your own medicine!'

Ripping off his tie, he used it to lasso the arm holding the bottle of pink medicine. Wrenching it upwards, he tore the bottle from the robot's grasp and promptly upended the medicine over its head. The liquid seeped into its joints, and sparks began to fly from the metal casing. The vile stuff had fried the robot's internal workings, including apparently its guidance system. Ryan leaped clear as M8-Tron spun round, out of control, arms clawing the air. It careened across the stage, and the Doctor neatly sidestepped out of its path.

The Faculty, however, was not so quick to react. The robot's flailing arms caught it, embracing it tight to its triangular chest.

'Oh, M8-Tron!'

As the two rolled past like a mismatched couple at a school dance, the Doctor stuck out a hand and nimbly plucked the keys from the Faculty's hip. Unable to stop themselves, M8-Tron and the Faculty trundled straight into the vacant airlock, triggering the automatic door mechanism as they crossed the threshold. The door closed with terrible finality, and the lock began to cycle. There was a hiss, as the outer door sprang open and a tongue of daylight poked inside. The outside air roiled like water during a frenzied piranha attack, and it seemed as if the very atmosphere bent and buckled as the shrieking Spectres poured through the gap, enveloping the Faculty and M8-Tron.

It was all over in a matter of seconds.

Sated after their feast, the Spectres retreated. The protective dome over Dorm reactivated, once more surrounding the school in its bubble.

A hush descended over the assembly hall. The Faculty's reign had come to an end.

The stunned silence was broken by a crackle of static over the school's public-address system, followed by an unfamiliar female voice.

'This is Earth Survey Ship *Guardian*, responding to your distress signal. We are three days out from your location. Heading to you now on maximum burn. Hang in there.'

A disbelieving murmur swept the hall. After all this time, someone was coming for them. Relief turned to tears for some of the younger children, while the older ones cheered, yanking off their ties and throwing them in the air.

Yaz appeared at the entrance to the hall. Making her way through the joyous celebrations, she joined the others and explained how she had found the communications centre and managed to send out the signal.

'Just goes to prove you should always read the manual,' she said.

'Funny. I don't think I've ever read one in my entire lives,' said the Doctor.

'Why doesn't that surprise me?' muttered Ryan.

The Doctor sifted through the keys she'd pinched from the Faculty. One was the same deep colour as the leaves of a copper beech tree, its blade engraved with a delicate leaf pattern.

'I think this is what we came for,' she said, holding it up.

'Then let's go,' said Graham. 'Clock's ticking on the Galactic Seed Vault.'

'Shouldn't we stay until the rescue ship gets here?' asked Yaz.

The Doctor looked around at the celebrating students of New Phaeton. 'No need. They're all going to be just fine. School's out. Forever.'

15. Exterminate

He was a mole-catcher, like his father, and his father before him. The Manners' family tradition extended into the past in an unbroken line, reaching back to the court of Henry VIII, when his ancestor held the title of Mole-catcher to the King.

These days, however, Tom Manners' clients were more likely to be wearing expensive suits than crowns. The only people who could afford gardens in London in 2018 were bankers, and today the job was one of those fancy residents-only gardens in Kensington. He'd had to park miles away, and it was a hot afternoon. 'Typical,' he grumbled to himself, as he checked the address again: Never Square. Not for the first time, he reflected on the oddity of the name.

He shifted the bag containing his traps from one shoulder to the other. It was getting heavy. The contents of the bag jangled. He'd brought six steel traps, all spring-loaded. Nowadays, though, he was just as likely to be asked to use humane traps and catch the mole without causing any harm. People were strange. The mole might be digging out a new Northern Line under their precious lawn, but still they went pale at the thought of exterminating the thing.

To Tom, moles were an enemy to be wiped out. Even so, he retained a healthy respect for the creatures. They were a formidable opponent; a perfectly adapted subterranean predator. Pound for pound, a mole could shift more earth than an excavator. The tunnels it clawed out – 'runs' in the professional lingo – were traps designed to catch earthworms, its primary food. A mole could sniff worms out as efficiently as a great white shark can smell a drop of blood in the ocean, and its saliva contained a poison that paralysed its prey, so that the mole could store the unfortunate worm in its larder to enjoy later as a midnight snack.

Tom had reached the address. The garden was ringed by high iron railings, and overshadowed by sweeping terraces of handsome white stucco townhouses. Tall sash windows with those little triangles of plaster above them gave the buildings the appearance of faces with raised eyebrows. Snooty, that's how Tom would describe them. From outside on the pavement, you wouldn't have known there was a garden not two metres away, since the residents had grown a tall hedge along the inside of the railings to stop anyone from being able to peek in.

Tom reread his instructions, which told him to go to the east gate. Like the railings, this gate was made of heavy black wrought iron and looked as if it could withstand a direct hit from a nuclear missile. He was no expert, but the gate looked old. Really old. It had a lock with a keyhole that'd take one of those big, heavy keys – the sort that jailers in a Dickens novel would carry around on a big metal band. The top half of the gate was decorated with a curious design. He had to squint against the brightness of the afternoon sun to make it out. Some kind of creature, curled around itself like a sleeping snake. Or maybe a dragon.

'Mr Manners?'

The voice startled him, and it took a moment before Tom realised it was coming from the very modern intercom attached to the ancient gate. The telltale lens of a camera scrutinised him.

'Yes, sir. That's me.'

'You are expected,' said the voice. Tom thought the man sounded like his old English teacher.

There was a click from the lock, then a long buzz. Tom pushed at the gate, and it swung open silently on oiled hinges. *Whoever looks after this place takes very good care of that gate*, he thought.

It was midsummer, and in the garden flower beds frothed with colour and the scent of roses drifted on the air. Tom made his way along a white gravel path, and each tiny stone looked as if it had been individually polished. The path led beneath an arched pergola, then wound past herbaceous borders and mature trees. He followed the snaking route, until the view opened up to reveal the heart of the garden.

Before him lay a broad expanse of lawn, shaded by three large oak trees and dotted with deckchairs, their stripy green-and-white seats stretched taut by a sudden and welcome breeze. In one corner overlooking the garden stood a stone statue of a man in a frock coat, with a severe expression and an exquisitely carved flower at his lapel. One of those little robotic lawnmowers buzzed up and down, keeping the short grass in perfect condition. Tom watched the mower trundle off and disappear behind the wide trunk of one of the oaks.

A second later, there came a thud.

Curious, Tom stepped past the tree to find the mower on its back, like some sort of mechanical beetle, wheels spinning uselessly in the air. On any other day, his first thought would have been to wonder how it had ended up like that, but he was distracted by something else: three mounds of freshly dug earth blotted the perfect lawn. They were each as wide as a manhole cover and as high as his hip. He set his bag of traps down next to the nearest mound, then crouched down to study it with professional interest. Whatever had made this, it was no mole. Certainly not any variety he – nor any of his illustrious ancestors, he'd bet – had ever come across.

He registered a flash of light in the corner of his eye and glanced round. It was just the sun reflecting off one of the townhouse windows, but he saw a figure standing in the window. As he watched, the figure closed a set of wooden shutters across the inside of the window. In the room above, another figure shuttered that window too. Tom was suddenly aware that, all around the square, shutters were closing across every window.

He shivered in the midsummer heat. *Come on, Tom*, he thought. *Get a grip, man.*

There was a jangle from behind him. His traps. Something had knocked the bag.

He turned to scan the garden, but couldn't see another soul. Actually, come to think of it, there was a distinct absence of wildlife too. For the first time, he noticed the complete lack of birdsong. *Probably can't afford the house prices round here*, he thought, turning back to the strange mounds of soil. As he did, he glimpsed the patch of grass at his feet. It had wobbled.

An instant later, Tom felt the ground beneath him give way. He dropped. A dark hole gaped in the lawn where, just moments ago, he had been standing.

His eyes opened slowly. He could only have been unconscious for a few seconds. As his vision gradually adjusted to his new surroundings, he saw he was underground, lying on the clammy earth floor of a tunnel the size of a sewer. Far above him, he could make out a small circle of daylight. He had fallen a surprisingly long way.

Must be an old mineshaft, he thought, anger building. As soon as he got out of there, he was going to send a complaint to the owners of Never Square. No, he would sue them!

He felt a throbbing at his temple. *Must have struck it on the way down*. He rubbed his head and tried to stand, but for some reason his legs wouldn't obey him.

His hand came away from his head wet. It was dripping with a sticky substance that he now realised was all over his clothes too. As he stared at his gloop-covered hand in the gloom, he heard a scuttling noise from somewhere in the darkness of the tunnel beyond.

He couldn't move. He was paralysed.

And that's when he knew: this was a run. And he was the worm.

The scuttling drew closer.

Ryan watched the TARDIS vanish into the afternoon. When the last wheezing groan had faded, he turned to follow Graham, who was already striding off along the pavement.

They'd decided to separate into pairs, in order to speed up their search for the two remaining keys to Vault Thirteen. He and Graham were back on earth in the present day, which had come as something of a let-down. Sure, things on New Phaeton had got a bit hairy, but Ryan was developing a taste for travelling to alien destinations with the Doctor.

According to the information stored on the navigational bluebell, the key that Ryan and Graham were after was hidden in some bloke's back garden. The most dangerous obstacle they'd encounter was likely to be an old guy shouting, 'Get off my lawn!'

'This is the place,' said Graham, pausing next to a black wrought-iron gate. 'Never Square.'

Ryan huffed. *Stupid name*. He was quite sure there was no chance of anything remotely exciting happening in a place like this.

16. Fantastic Voyage

'Has it broken down again?' Yaz waited for the Doctor to respond, but she didn't seem to hear, being too busy inspecting the TARDIS systems for faults.

Less than five minutes ago, they'd dropped Ryan and Graham off in London. The TARDIS had dematerialised as normal, but soon after that their journey had come to a stuttering halt. Now, they appeared to be stuck.

The external scanner showed them drifting in the sparkling cosmos. Gazing at the endless star field, Yaz was reminded of a school camping trip she'd gone on to the Dales one year. She and her best friend, Aisha, had shared a tent, and out in the wilds of the national park they'd marvelled at the vastness of the night sky, but it paled in comparison with the view in front of her now. That night on the camping trip, Aisha had decided to become an astronaut. What would she make of Yaz now, out here among the stars?

'How odd,' said the Doctor at last. 'Everything appears to be working. At least as much as usual.' She rapped the console. 'What are you up to? Hmm?'

Yaz had noticed that the Doctor often addressed the TARDIS as if it was a person. That wasn't so strange; her mum once had a Fiat called Pavarotti.

'Since the TARDIS doesn't appear to want to budge, I'll just have to input the location of the next key and fly us there myself,' the Doctor said.

Yaz picked up the navigational bluebell containing the time-and-space co-ordinates of the three keys, and offered it to her.

'I may be brilliant,' said the Doctor, 'but I can't read an encrypted bluebell. Happily, the TARDIS has already downloaded the information, so I'm going to just hook myself up to its telepathic circuits and go for a rummage. Fancy coming along?'

'You're going inside the TARDIS? Like, inside its mind?' That sounded awesome. 'Of course I want to come.'

The Doctor spun a knob. 'Used to be that, to access the circuits, you shoved your hands into a blob of telepathic gel, but that was *not* hygienic.'

As the Doctor slowly pulled the knob out, Yaz saw that it was attached to a long, slim metal rod that ended in a gleaming point. It was the hypodermic needle of her nightmares.

'Now I'm just going to stick this –'

'No way!' Yaz threw up her hands and backed away.

'In here,' said the Doctor, reaching past Yaz to insert the device into another section of the vessel's labyrinthine machinery.

'Oh,' said Yaz, abashed but nonetheless wary. 'Going into the TARDIS like this – does it hurt?'

'No. *No.* Well, maybe just a smidge. I mean, it's not like mentally duelling the brain of Morbius was. That stung like a helmet full of wasps. But, on the flip side, it isn't like looking for a clean pair of pants in your bottom drawer, either.' She waggled her hand in a gesture of approximation. 'Somewhere between the two, agony-wise.'

'Agony? You didn't say anything about ag–'

Suddenly the TARDIS pitched over, throwing Yaz across the room. She hit the floor and slid along it, until she thumped against the wall. Picking herself up, she checked for bruises and saw that, remarkably, the Doctor had remained upright. She seemed to sense Yaz's puzzlement.

'Nadia Comăneci, first gymnast to achieve a perfect ten when she was at the 1976 Olympics,' she said by way of explanation. 'Taught me how to stick the landing.'

The TARDIS shook again, more violently this time. Yaz grabbed the edge of the wall and held on. A third blast plunged them briefly into darkness, before the interior of the TARDIS filled with soft blue light.

'Emergency lighting,' said the Doctor.

'I thought emergency lighting was always red,' said Yaz.

'It's an emergency, Yaz. You don't want to alarm people.' Her hands skimmed the controls and the external scanner bloomed into life, displaying an image of the surrounding space.

What looked like a vast log drifted past, gnarled and scored with gouges. *A fragment of intergalactic driftwood*, Yaz figured, but then she saw the spire of a radar dish poking up from the middle, and the vivid yellow glow of engines.

'It's a ship,' she said.

'Gardener warship, if I'm not mistaken,' said the Doctor. 'It's not all about wheelbarrows with them. Their sun-drives use an advanced form of photosynthesis to transform light into fuel for faster-than-light travel. But how did they find us? The chances of their ship being in the same space at the same time as the TARDIS are astronomically – and chronologically – small.'

An arc of green fire leaped from the midship, and the TARDIS shuddered again. A warning light began flashing. This was not the moment to speculate on how the Gardeners had tracked them down.

'We've lost time-travel propulsion,' said the Doctor. 'I should be able to get it working again, but in the meantime I'll have to outrun them in regular space.' She adjusted the control settings, diverting power for the impending chase. 'You'll have to go in alone.'

'Go in where?' Yaz was briefly stumped, then she understood. 'The TARDIS?'

With one hand, the Doctor steered out of the path of another blast from the Gardener warship. With the other hand, she withdrew the needle and offered it to Yaz. It glowed with a blue light similar in hue to the one on top of the

TARDIS. 'Hold this with both hands,' she instructed.

'How is this going to help?'

'Have you heard of dowsing rods? Sometimes called divining rods. On earth they were an ancient method of detecting water beneath the ground by waving sticks around.'

That seemed unlikely. 'Did it work?' Yaz asked.

'Surprisingly often.' The Doctor thrust the needle at her. 'You're going dowsing for the co-ordinates of the next key. When you're ready, clasp the needle.'

As Yaz reached out, the Doctor snatched it away. 'Couple of points to bear in mind before you begin. You're going to see things. They're going to feel real. They *are* real, but they're also constructs formed from memories and thoughts. And one more thing.' Her tone darkened. 'These telepathic circuits are connected to the TARDIS's navigational function, so your timeline might get a little jumbled. Beginnings, middles and endings mean diddly-squat to a time machine. But almost certainly nothing to worry about.'

She smiled and proffered the needle once more. 'Ready?'

'No.' Yaz reached out and wrapped her fingers round the needle just as the TARDIS was struck again. The console exploded into flames, and the room disappeared.

'Hey, Yazzer, what're you doing in here?'

Yaz blinked. Before her slouched a twelve-year-old girl in a school uniform and a hijab. She briefly glanced up from her mobile phone.

'Aisha?' What was her best friend from school doing aboard the TARDIS? Yaz glanced around. She was in the girls' cloakroom of her secondary school. Except it wasn't, of course. It was – what had the Doctor called it? – a construct. She inhaled the musty scent of wet woollen coats. Uncanny. She reached out and stroked the imaginary Aisha's cheek, gently pinching it between finger and thumb.

Aisha slapped her hand away. 'Weirdo.'

The back of her hand smarted and she was struck by a disconcerting thought. She ran to Carly Green's locker and wrenched it open. Even though it was against the school rules, Carly had taped a mirror to the inside of the door. Yaz gazed into it.

She was twelve years old again.

Breathing heavily, she flopped down on the bench and put her head in her hands. There was another explanation for what was going on: perhaps all of *this* was real, and she'd just woken up from the strangest dream of her life. After all, what was more likely to be true? That she was a twenty-year-old travelling the universe with a Time Lord in a police box, or that she was twelve and at school in Sheffield? Maybe she'd banged her head and was suffering from a concussion. Or she'd eaten something weird. On a dare, Gary Clark in Year Eight had eaten a really hot chilli pepper and hallucinated that he was a French-speaking penguin. Maybe the same thing had happened to her? But that would mean there was no Doctor, no TARDIS, no Galactic Seed Vault.

The vault!

She remembered why she was there.

There was an intrusive click-clicking and something blurred in front of her nose. Her eyes swam back into focus to see Aisha snapping her fingers.

'Hey, space cadet,' said her friend. 'What is up with you today?'

'I didn't eat a chilli,' she said.

'You what?'

'I'm looking for something.'

'Yeah, your mind, which you appear to have lost.'

'Come on, you can help. I have a feeling you're here for a reason.' She grabbed Aisha by the arm and hustled her out of the cloakroom. They took one step over the threshold, then stopped abruptly, as though they'd come to the edge of the world.

'Whoa!'

'Uh, where's the rest of the school?' asked Aisha.

Instead of the science corridor, they were standing on the roof of a skyscraper, looking out over what at first glance appeared to be a big city at night. Lights pulsed in the darkness like traffic on a motorway.

'Those aren't cars,' said Yaz. 'I think they're my memories.' They zipped up and down neural pathways, forming and re-forming. 'We're in my mind.'

'Can't be,' said Aisha. 'It's too big.'

Yaz ignored the barb. 'This is no good. The location of the key isn't in my mind. I need to get inside the TARDIS.'

The two girls descended to street level, and set off along the byways of Yaz's mind, passing thoughts she hadn't had in years.

'Look!' she exclaimed. 'Calculating the area of parallelograms and trapeziums.' It lay there unopened, like a piece of junk mail. And it was not alone. She blew the dust off another unloved thought. 'Fronted adverbials.'

'Your mind is even untidier than your bedroom,' said Aisha. 'Where are we going now?'

'There,' said Yaz. Up ahead lay the local park. 'We didn't have a garden, so we used to play here all the time. Remember?'

'Of course I remember. We were here yesterday.'

They ran through the open gates and followed the path past the swings and roundabout to a quiet clearing among a stand of trees. A broad old chestnut tree swayed in the wind, its branches thick with spiky green husks.

Yaz studied the memory. 'Remember when we sat under this tree to do our homework?'

'Yeah, I remember I did *my* homework. Not sure what you were doing.'

On the ground lay dozens of fallen husks, some split open to reveal glossy red-brown conkers. And, among the fallen fruit, nestled at the base of the trunk, something fluttered in the breeze. It was Yaz's old homework book.

She picked it up and flicked through pages filled with her childish scrawl. It was her maths homework. At school she'd liked numbers, but hadn't been sure the feeling was mutual. She stopped at a swirlingly complex algebra equation far beyond anything she could recall ever learning. It wasn't her handwriting. Someone else had inserted it here. Could this be the information she was searching for?

She stared hard at the equation, willing it to make sense, but it was no use. Then she had an idea. 'Aisha, you were always better at this stuff than me.'

'No kidding,' said her friend. 'Y'know, when I'm not appearing in your flashbacks, I'm now an aerospace engineer.' She examined the page. 'Right, what have we got here?'

'Is it a set of co-ordinates?' Yaz asked hopefully.

Aisha scanned the page. 'Not exactly. More like directions. How to get from here to the TARDIS.'

Finally, Yaz was on the right track. With Aisha to decipher the directions, she'd soon be in possession of the vital information.

The trunk of the chestnut tree moved. A figure made of bark detached itself, and a secateurs-like hand swiped at Yaz. She ducked and took a step back. It was a Gardener. Here, in her mind.

'Run!' As she turned to flee, she almost tripped over something on the ground. Glancing down, she saw that it was the Doctor. She was sprawled full-length in the grass, unmoving, her eyes wide open but empty. Giving no thought to the advancing Gardener, Yaz dropped to her knees and pressed a palm to the Doctor's chest, first one side then the other, searching for either heartbeat. Nothing.

'Come on!' Aisha grabbed Yaz, and hauled her away.

They fled through a wood, and Yaz glanced back in horror. Behind them, the Gardener was standing over the Doctor's motionless body, like a hunter with their prize. Bizarrely, flakes of snow were falling on the Gardener and the Doctor.

There was no doubt in Yaz's mind. The Doctor was dead.

She had told Yaz that things could get jumbled up in here, that being connected to the TARDIS's time circuits might affect the order of events. Everything she'd seen until now had already happened – from Aisha to the park to her homework. That could leave only one terrible conclusion.

I think I just saw the future.

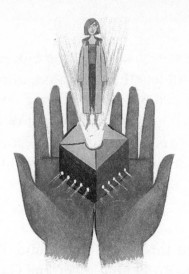

17. Party Animal

Though the Doctor hadn't accompanied Ryan and Graham, she had sent them to earth with what she called 'the second-best thing – okay, maybe the third'. They had been in the TARDIS wardrobe, finding suitable outfits for the upcoming mission, when she presented it to them. It was a palm-sized cube constructed from some kind of white plastic, and if Ryan was honest it looked a bit rubbish.

'It's me,' the Doctor had explained, 'but in portable form.'

Ryan regarded the white cube doubtfully. 'Doesn't look like you.'

'It's programmed with knowledge gained from all of my regenerations. Well, at least as much as you can fit into thirty-two brontobytes of memory. It's just the entry-level cube. The cost of brontobyte storage is exorbitant.' She held it up and a light pulsed inside. 'If you come up against anything you don't understand, or if you need advice, just ask the mysterious glowing cube.' She tossed it to Ryan. 'You activate it with the phrase "Okay, Doctor". Go on, try it out.'

'Okay, Doctor.'

In response, the cube had glowed and a tiny holographic image of the Doctor appeared on the top surface and began to speak in her voice. 'Hello, Ryan. I'm listening.'

He'd known exactly what to ask. Finally, an opportunity to pose the question that had been bugging him since he'd joined her crew. 'What is the correct sequence of controls for starting the TARDIS?'

The hologram Doctor had answered instantly. 'Cream the butter and sugar together, beat in the eggs, sift over the flour and fold in to the mixture –'

'I think that's the method for sponge cake,' Yaz had said.

The Doctor had grabbed the cube and given it a vigorous shake. 'Yes, it can be a little erratic at times.'

Now, the cube lay on his open palm, as he waited for Graham outside the locked gate of the residents-only garden on Never Square. Graham had gone in search of an alternate way in, figuring that the owners weren't likely to open up to a couple of complete strangers. Ryan decided to consult the cube.

'Okay, Doctor.'

On cue, the cube glowed and the mini-Doctor appeared. 'Hello, Ryan. I'm listening.'

'What's the best way to get in here?'

'The best way to remove stains from wool is with a lint-free cloth dipped in a solution of equal parts alcohol and white vinegar.'

Talk about a useless gadget.

'What's that thing?' said a small voice from behind the fence railings.

Ryan looked up. The owner of the voice was a boy of around seven or eight years old. He was a slight child with a pale complexion, and when he spoke there was a high pitch to his voice that was, to be frank, instantly annoying. He was dressed in an oddly formal manner for someone so young. Since it was summer, most kids were in T-shirts and shorts, but the boy sported a stiff white shirt tucked into a pair of neatly pressed grey trousers and polished brogues. He peered out at Ryan, curious eyes fixed on the cube.

Thankfully, the hologram of the Doctor had vanished, making Ryan's explanation simpler. 'It's a portable speaker,' he said, pocketing the device and walking up to the railings. 'What's your name?'

'Jonathan. What's yours?'

'I'm Ryan,' he said. 'Can you let me in?'

'You don't want to come in here, trust me. We were expecting two guests for the feast, but one didn't show up. So there's a lot of shouting. Father is a-po-plec-tic.' He carefully pronounced each syllable. 'That means his head's about to explode, he's so angry. Unless . . .' The boy thought for a moment. 'Would you like to come to the feast?'

Dinner or a party, thought Ryan. That explained the boy's fancy get-up. If the invitation would get him inside, he wasn't going to turn it down. 'You are looking at a regular party animal,' he said.

A smile spread across the boy's face, and he unlocked the gate. 'Father will be pleased.'

He was in. Now to find the second key. Maybe it was hanging up in a shed, or perhaps it was the key to one of the garden gates? He kept his eyes peeled, only half listening to the boy's incessant chat, as they walked along a white gravel path. It seemed Ryan's presence was a bit of a novelty. Maybe Jonathan didn't get out much.

They hadn't gone far, when their route was blocked by Alice in Wonderland. At least, that's who she looked like to Ryan. She occupied the centre of the path, wearing a pale blue dress and party shoes. A hairband held a wave of blonde hair off her face, which was wearing an expression of annoyance. She folded her arms and tapped one foot on the ground. On second thought, maybe more Queen of Hearts than Alice.

'My sister,' muttered Jonathan.

Ryan didn't have a sister, but he did have Yaz and he'd seen the same disapproving expression on her face.

'Who's this?' the girl said. She obviously meant Ryan, but her gaze was fixed on her little brother.

'He's my friend.'

'I'm here for the party,' said Ryan.

'He means the feast,' said Jonathan.

'Oh.' The girl seemed surprised. 'Aren't you a little on the skinny side?'

Jonathan lowered his head and pushed past her, dragging Ryan behind. 'Ignore her,' he muttered. 'She's always going on at me. Do you have pets?'

'Uh, no,' he said. 'But my granddad has a begonia.'

'A begonia isn't a pet.'

'You haven't met this one.'

Jonathan angled off the path, ducking through a gap in the shrubbery. Ryan trailed after him, elbowing his way through the bushes to emerge in a clearing on the other side. Between two flower beds was a raised patch of grass, bowed up in the centre like a humpback bridge.

Ryan looked around for a hutch. 'So what have you got? Rabbits? Guinea pigs?'

'Something much better. Doctor Never brought it back from one of his expeditions.'

Ryan stopped himself from making a lame dad joke about him being Doctor No's cousin.

'When it first arrived in the garden, it could fit in his hand. But that was a long time ago. Even then it was vo-ra-cious. That means it had a big appetite. Doctor Never tried to get rid of it, but it was too late.'

'Eat too many carrots, did it?' Pets were expensive. Ryan had never been allowed one for that very reason.

'At first, he tried to make it leave, but that didn't work. It only made it sad. So he carried on feeding it, to keep it happy. It likes me, I think because I'm the one who brings it food.'

Ryan had about had enough of the boy's weird and also rather dull pet story. He wasn't here to look at fluffy animals; he had a job to do. 'Listen, Jonathan. I need your help. This is serious.'

The boy paused and looked up at him expectantly.

'I'm searching for a key,' Ryan said. 'A very special one. It might be made of gold, or it might look like a regular, y'know, key. Someone hid it in your garden, and it's very important that I find it. Quickly. So, if you have any idea –'

Jonathan nodded. 'I know exactly where it is.'

Well, that was a stroke of luck! The Doctor would be impressed when Ryan produced the second key in less time than it'd take to travel from one end of the universe to the other in a TARDIS. 'That's great. Good lad. I mean, good for you. So, show me.'

Jonathan swept back a flowering branch that had fallen over what Ryan now saw was a short flight of worn steps that led down into the grassy hump. The two of them descended,

Jonathan's shoes making a hollow clicking sound on the stone steps.

At the bottom of the stairs, there was just enough daylight to make out a small space with a soil floor and a low, arched ceiling fashioned from corrugated iron. A wooden bench sat against one wall.

'It's called an Anderson shelter,' explained Jonathan. 'It's an old air-raid shelter from the war. Lots of bombs were dropped on London during the Blitz, and the people who lived here used to hide in this shelter during the raids. Never Square was hit four times.'

'I'm surprised it's still here.' Ryan tried to picture a family huddled in the shelter, taking refuge from Nazi bombs.

'That's because not all the bombs went off. They found one of them a few years ago, buried in a flower bed. UXB. It stands for unexploded bomb. Can you imagine something so deadly lurking just under your feet all that time?' Then the boy gave a small chuckle.

Ryan looked around. At some point since the war the shelter had been turned into a garden shed and a dumping ground. Broken flowerpots lay strewn across the soil floor, and a rusting rake and a handful of other tools were propped against one wall. A colony of insects had taken up residence in a pair of worn gardening gloves. On the floor next to the gloves sat a surprisingly new LED lamp designed to look like an old-fashioned storm lantern. Unlike the rest of the dust-laden objects in here, it looked as if it had been in use recently.

'So where's my key, Jonathan?'

'It's close,' he said, clicking on the lamp. It spread a cool, blue light into the corners of the shelter, illuminating a section low down in the back wall that appeared to be a hatch. It was held loosely in place by a handful of screws. Jonathan unscrewed them, and removed the hatch.

Ryan was immediately hit by a waft of stale air mixed with something more pungent. The sharp stink of fox or some other wild animal, perhaps.

Jonathan raised the lantern and, on hands and knees, scrambled through the gap beneath the hatch.

Ryan watched the light fade into the darkness beyond. This would certainly make a good hiding place for a legendary key.

'Well, come on,' urged Jonathan. 'What are you waiting for?'

Ryan squeezed through the hatch, and was surprised to find himself in a tunnel made of compacted earth, with a roof high enough that he was able to stand up. The tunnel appeared to slope gently downwards. Jonathan's swinging lantern was already several metres ahead, lighting the gloom, and Ryan hurried to catch up.

'So what's the tunnel for?' he asked the boy. 'Was it built as part of the air-raid shelter?'

'No, silly,' said Jonathan with a breathy giggle. 'I told you.'

By the lantern light, Ryan noticed that Jonathan's shirt was flecked with mud where he'd brushed up against the soil. So was his face. Streaks of mud decorated his cheeks and forehead like a tiger's stripes. The marks were too deliberate – the boy must have applied them to himself.

'What are you talking about?' Away from the warmth of the summer's day outside, Ryan suddenly felt cold. 'What did you tell me?'

'That we needed two guests for the feast, but only one showed up.'

From somewhere along the tunnel came a scuttling that shook the walls. Loosened by the vibration, beads of mud dribbled down the sides. Ryan felt a prickling at the nape of his neck. 'What was that?'

With a grin, Jonathan raised the lantern. At the very limit of its illumination, Ryan glimpsed something in the tunnel. Something monstrous.

'Father *will* be pleased.'

18. Unearthly Child's Play

Yaz was stuck in her own head, but she was supposed to be in the TARDIS's. This wasn't like previous occasions, such as when she couldn't escape her anxiety about a forthcoming exam or shake off a persistent song lyric. No. This time, she was literally stuck. In her head.

The Doctor had sent her to dredge up the co-ordinates of the third key from the TARDIS's circuits, but so far all she'd accomplished was a reunion with her best friend from school. They'd been following the directions in her homework book, when Aisha had vanished like a dream in the morning, leaving Yaz alone in some kind of limbo. Where before she had been surrounded by artefacts of her own history, thoughts and moments endlessly replayed in her mind, now she was engulfed in darkness. A non-place. She hung in the void like an untethered astronaut in space. At least she was no longer twelve years old – once was quite enough.

She cupped a hand to her mouth and called out, 'Doctor! Can you hear me?'

No reply, except for the faint echo of her own voice.

How was she going to get back to the TARDIS now? If she was Dorothy from *The Wizard of Oz* she could have clicked her heels together three times. She glanced down. Clicking was trickier in trainers. As she stared at her shoes, a round, glowing disc formed beneath her feet, the universe tilted and she tumbled away, landing a moment later with a thud on the bare floor of a brightly lit corridor.

It was the TARDIS. She'd made it.

The walls curved up and around her, their smooth silver surface interrupted at regular intervals by glowing rounds like the one she'd glimpsed a second ago. Or was it an hour ago? The passage of time was tricky to measure. The silent corridor stretched out before her, the repeating pattern on the wall vanishing into the distance. She looked over her shoulder. It was the same in that direction.

Seeing no other option, she began to walk. Somewhere in here was the information she needed. But where? After a while, she began to wonder if the straightness of the corridor was an illusion and in fact she was going round in – her eye caught the pattern once more – circles.

She decided to test her theory. Her plan was simple: scratch a mark into one of the discs, then keep walking. If she encountered the mark again, she'd know the true nature of the corridor. All she needed was something to make a mark with. Unlike the Doctor, she didn't carry a handy sonic screwdriver. She used to keep a spare key to her flat and a couple of bank cards in her wallet, but she'd stopped taking the wallet out with her since almost losing it on a Martian moon base in the year 3049. That would've been a tough call to the bank's helpline.

With low expectations, she delved into her pockets, and was surprised when her fingers clutched something cold and hard.

It was a small silver key. The one that opened her flat's front door.

She had no recollection of putting it in her pocket. All the talk of keys must have affected her, and this must be another of those imaginary constructs the Doctor had warned her about. No matter. It would do. If she was trapped in some diabolical mind-maze, this would prove it. She pressed the point of the key to a disc on the wall.

'Won't work,' said a voice.

Yaz jumped, startled. She looked round to see a boy, around nine years old, leaning against the wall with his arms folded. She squinted at him in disbelief.

'Ryan?'

19. By-laws

Graham helped himself to another mini mushroom Wellington and observed the partygoers with quiet satisfaction. Men in grey suits and women in summer dresses enjoyed drinks on the lawn, their polite burble of conversation accompanied by the tinkle of cut-crystal glasses and the pop of champagne corks. Honeyed music played by a string quartet swooned over the garden, while waiters glided among the guests, offering up silver trays laden with canapés. As the evening light faded, two waiters set flaming wooden torches into the ground, filling the garden with flickering light.

So far, so good. Graham's ruse had worked, and he'd made it inside. At first, he'd gone back for Ryan, but couldn't find him so decided to press on with the mission. The boy was resourceful – he'd probably made it into the garden already. Graham was sure they'd be reunited very soon.

He looked around at the assembled guests, and congratulated himself on his deception. It was brilliantly simple, really. Half of the houses round the square were empty, their international owners rarely there to occupy them. They were investments, not places to live. He'd found one such house, identified by the mailbox overflowing with unopened mail, made a note of the name and pretended to be a cousin. He'd convinced the host of the party, Mr Delgado, with surprising ease. Delgado struck him as an agreeable man, not keen to cause a scene at the residents' summer bash by turning away an uninvited guest.

There was just one minor drawback to Graham's ploy. The name on the mailbox had been Ivanov, which meant he'd had to adopt a Russian persona. He'd put on an accent and felt fairly confident that he sounded Russian, but there was a chance he was coming across as Welsh.

He polished off another canapé and took a tiny sip of champagne. He needed to keep a clear head if he was going to track down the second key. He knew it was close, but where exactly?

He scanned the garden and the guests. Most were chatting, while a few listened to the music. A couple of the men had discarded their jackets, rolled up their sleeves and, by the light of the torches, were using a hammer to bang a wooden post into the lawn between the three heaped mounds of earth. The other guests ignored the report of hammer strikes. Briefly, Graham wondered if it was some kind of maypole that they would dance round later. Or perhaps it was part of a very big croquet set.

A statue in the far corner of the garden caught his eye, and he forgot all about the men with the hammer. He drew closer. The stone figure looked like a typical Edwardian worthy, but there was something about the way he held out his hands that didn't make sense. They grasped thin air. As if something was missing from their grip.

'Ah, there you are, Mr Asimov!' Delgado's voice hailed him from across the lawn.

Graham turned to see him approaching, accompanied by another guest. Like the rest of the male guests, the men wore sober suits and the residents'-association tie. Delgado sported a beard and moustache as neatly trimmed as one of his prize hedges, while the other man was bald as an egg. Delgado gestured towards the statue. 'I see you've discovered our founder, Doctor Never.'

'*Da, da,*' said Graham, using the only Russian word he knew. 'Was he ze even more evil cousin of Doctor No?' He attempted a deep chortle, and was answered by blank looks from the two men. He cleared his throat and raised his champagne flute for another sip.

'The good doctor was a plant collector,' Delgado said, his eyes fixed on the statue. 'Went all over the world bringing back rare and exotic species. Sometimes not just the flora, but the fauna too. Over the years, he returned from his travels with many strange and wonderful beasts. You'd be amazed at what kind of creatures still exist in the so-called modern world.'

Graham paid little attention to Delgado; he had more important things on his mind. 'It seems as if ze statue should be holding something. Do you know vot?'

'Well spotted,' said Delgado. 'Yes, it was a key.'

The second key. It had to be! Graham tried not to show his excitement. 'And vot became of zis key?'

Delgado made a face. 'No idea, old chap. There are photographs in the archives that show it as part of the statue, but at some point over the years it went missing. Why the interest?'

Graham thought desperately for a sensible answer. 'I am a collector too . . . of keys. *Da.* Anything with keys.' What was he saying? 'Keys, keyboards . . .' *Shut up now, Graham.* 'Monkeys.' He smiled awkwardly, and drained the rest of his champagne.

Delgado exchanged a puzzled look with the bald man. Then, as if he had just remembered why he was there, he introduced the bald man. 'Mr Asimov, may I present a compatriot of yours. This is Professor Tarkovsky.'

Graham almost spat out his champagne. This was bad. He could just about fool another Brit with his dodgy accent, but there was no way he'd get away with it in front of an actual Russian person. He was just wondering how to dig himself out this hole when Delgado added, 'He is also Mr Ivanov's *real* cousin.'

Caught red-handed, Graham braced himself for the inevitable accusations, perhaps even the threat of the police, certainly the immediate prospect of being kicked out of the garden. But Delgado was interrupted by another guest

196

whispering in his ear. He smiled and turned to Graham. 'It seems we're ready for you.'

Before Graham could ask what was going on, he felt hands grip him and pin his arms to his sides. Protesting, he was half carried through the crowd, the guests parting to create a corridor of leering faces at the end of which loomed the wooden post. Since he'd last looked, the post had gained a heavy chain and manacles. Delgado signalled to one of the men, who clamped the manacles to Graham's ankle. He felt it bite.

'Hey! Get it off me! What is this? You're all crazy!' His objections went ignored. Whatever was going on, everyone here was in on it. He raised his voice to shout for help, hoping to be heard on the street beyond the garden, but the string quartet played louder to drown him out. He noticed that the musicians had changed their tune. In place of genteel chamber music, they now played something altogether less harmonious. The violins screeched like the cry of some injured animal, and Graham found himself panting quickly in time to the terrible, primal rhythm.

Mr Delgado collected a handful of loose soil from one of the nearby mounds and, using a finger, streaked his own cheeks and forehead.

As Graham looked around, he saw the other guests doing the same.

Delgado turned his back on Graham and threw up his arms. Instantly the music faded to a background murmur, and he began to address the other residents. Graham could have shouted for help now, but he was transfixed by Delgado's words.

'We are gathered here today to give thanks to the One That Lurks,' he began.

'The One That Lurks,' echoed the guests.

What was he on about? Graham wanted to believe he was the subject of a cruel prank, but something about Delgado's tone made him suspect otherwise. A few clumps of earth trickled down the side of the nearest mound of soil.

'For more than a hundred years, the residents of Never Square have lived side by side with our neighbour, in peace and harmony. We enjoy these splendid houses, this beautiful garden, affordable council tax, convenient residents' parking, and the wonderful amenities of the borough. All our neighbour asks in return is our annual gift. Tonight, we give it. But, first, in accordance with the time-honoured ritual, let us recite the sacred by-laws.' He drew breath and intoned, 'The garden is reserved for the exclusive use of rate-paying owners.'

The residents repeated the line.

'Children under ten must be accompanied by an adult.'

They repeated that too.

Delgado continued to list more rules, and the residents echoed each one back to him. 'No football at any time. Dogs shall not be allowed on weekends. Barbecues must only be lit in designated areas. The flesh of two men must be offered up for the annual feast.'

Graham snapped bolt upright. 'Beg your pardon?'

It appeared that he'd fallen into the clutches of some weird cannibal cult. In Kensington.

'Bring the additional tribute,' Delgado commanded, and one of the guests stepped forward. For some inexplicable reason, she was holding a shiny chrome espresso maker. She thrust it into Graham's hands. What the – ? Was he about to be sacrificed to a demonic barista?

Delgado turned slowly to face him again. 'Neighbour, we consign the flesh of this man to you so that you may sleep with a full belly for another year, and we –'

'Father, stop!'

The crowd parted to let through a young boy and girl. The boy was wide-eyed with excitement, the girl's expression sullen.

'Jonathan,' said Delgado tightly. 'This is not the time.'

'I told you,' said the girl.

'But I found him,' said the boy. 'The second guest for the feast. I took him below.' His face fell. 'I thought you'd be pleased.'

Graham seized his opportunity. 'Second guest? So that means you've already got two men, right?'

The boy nodded, pleased that someone appreciated his efforts.

Delgado remained silent, thrown by the unexpected development. A ripple of uncertainty went through the rest of the residents.

Graham adjusted his grip on the espresso maker. It was heavier than it looked. He pushed home his argument. 'Your by-laws state that the annual feast consists of the flesh of two men. Not three. So that means –'

Delgado had clearly made a decision. He waved a hand at the quartet, and they struck up again with their strange, pulsing music. Graham was drowned out once more, but he clung to the hope that he had the by-laws on his side. A hope that lasted little longer than ten seconds, when the ground beneath his feet began to tremble.

He could feel something powerful thrumming just below the earth's surface. Whatever it was seemed to be drawn by the music. He swallowed.

Or perhaps it was attracted by the scent of human flesh? He glanced down in time to see a grotesque snout burst out of the lawn, pink and glistening, a wriggling star-shaped thing with wormy feelers. It was attached to a creature the size of a grizzly bear, with matted, stinking fur and dirty claw-like hands that would have seemed comically oversized for its body if they hadn't been so terrifyingly close to him.

The creature's arrival sent clumps of earth and stones flying. Its alien mouth gaped, and Graham let out a scream. The giant claws embraced him, he heard the snap of the chain that bound him to the post, and just before he blacked out he felt himself being pulled underground.

20. A Hiccup in Time

It was Ryan, all right. Looking just the same as he had when they were at school together. He was dressed in a blue T-shirt, blue jeans and blue trainers. TARDIS blue. The ship had plundered her memory again. Like Aisha, he was a friendly face that the timeship was using to communicate with her.

Ryan didn't seem such an odd choice for the Doctor's space–time machine. In her experience, nine-year-old children were restless, curious, strong-willed, often reluctant to do exactly what they were told or go where they were meant to, but fiercely loyal and with hearts far bigger than their outward appearance would suggest. Maybe a good fit after all. She decided to go along with the latest puppet show.

'Why won't it work?' she asked, holding up the key with which she'd intended to mark the disc on the wall.

'I already tried,' he said. 'I've been stuck in here for ages. The mark is always gone the next time you enter the corridor.'

'So it *is* the same corridor?'

'I'm pretty sure,' said Ryan. 'Sometimes it's bright and endlessly long, other times it can be dark and a dead end. It's a passage aboard an alien space station, or a burrow belonging to some subterranean creature. It's on Skaro and on Gallifrey. But, yeah, it's always the same corridor.'

Yaz didn't know what to think. She was in a corridor. *The* corridor, apparently. 'Does it lead to the key to Vault Thirteen?'

'I guess it must, eventually,' said Ryan. 'Everything's in here.'

'What do you mean "everything"?'

'You'll see,' he said, a smile flitting across his face.

She wasn't in the mood for riddles. 'I've got to find that key. You know how important it is. The TARDIS was supposed to take us to its location.'

'Maybe it did.'

This was infuriating. 'But it didn't go anywhere.'

Ryan shrugged. 'Do you remember what Mrs Knowles always used to say?'

Old Know-It-All Knowles was a teacher from primary school. Not one of Yaz's fonder memories. 'Uh . . . "That is your last warning, young lady"?'

'Yes, but there was something else.'

'Are you going to tell me or not?' she snapped at Ryan.

'She said, "Stop thinking about where you're going. Focus on what's right in front of you."'

'Oh, come on!'

'I didn't say she was original.' He folded his arms in a grump. 'And, anyway, she's *your* memory.'

Yaz had endured quite enough of TARDIS Ryan. 'If that's all I'm getting from you, then I'm out of here. Where's the door?'

'Ah.'

'What does that mean?'

'There is no door. You're stuck.'

The corridor shook, and Yaz stumbled, just managing to stay on her feet.

'The TARDIS is still under attack,' said Ryan. 'Lots of its systems are malfunctioning, including the one that put you in here. The Doctor is doing what she can out there –' he pointed vaguely above his head – 'but she's also trying to outrun that warship.'

The mention of the Doctor was a sharp reminder to Yaz. 'I saw something. The Doctor. She was dead.'

The mask slipped and the TARDIS's true face showed through. 'Yes, she does that.'

'Was it real?'

'Define real?'

'I mean, did it – will it – happen?'

TARDIS Ryan cocked his head to one side and regarded her with a mixture of curiosity and pity. 'It must be so confusing for you, having to exist with such a basic understanding of time. I mean, you still believe in all that past, present and future stuff, don't you?'

'What other way is there?'

'I'd tell you, but your brain is too simple an organism to contain the ideas. It might explode.' He grinned, evidently intrigued by the grisly prospect. 'It's a bit like hiccups,' he said.

For a moment, Yaz thought he was referring to the incomprehensible theory of time he'd alluded to.

'What's gone wrong with the telepathic circuits,' he clarified. 'Except that hiccups don't usually drive you insane.'

'Is that what's going to happen to me?'

'Oh, at the very least. Certainly if we can't get you out of the TARDIS circuits before the Doctor is forced to travel in time again. Which she must – and soon. It will come down to a choice: you, or the fate of the universe. Same old, same old.'

Yaz swallowed hard. 'Better find me a glass of water then.'

'That doesn't cure hiccups. It's a myth.' He turned his back and began to walk off along the corridor. 'No, there's only one proven way to get rid of them.'

'What's that then?'

He paused, then spoke without looking at her. 'I'm going to scare you out of your skin.'

21. Kensington Gore

Ryan returned to consciousness with a great gulp.

He immediately wished he hadn't. It was the smell that hit him first: the same stink he'd detected at the entrance to the tunnel, but much stronger here. The stench of death. It poured into his nostrils, making him gag. Jonathan's lantern lay a few metres away, casting a pool of light over a boneyard. Pale white shards littered the earth. Skeletal fingers poked up through the soil floor, twisted, snapped, licked clean. The smooth ball of a thigh bone was a blank, one-eyed stare in the darkness.

Ryan was in no doubt that these were the remains of victims devoured by the creature that had attacked him in the tunnel. The same fate awaited him unless he could find a way out of this place. He strained to hear in the dank silence. Nothing but the faintest suggestion of . . . violins?

At least the monster wasn't in here with him – for now. He tried to move, but met resistance. He was wrapped up to the neck in a hard shell of dried mud, his body cocooned so tightly he couldn't feel his limbs. He calmed himself with a series of deep breaths, and his mind flitted back to the terrible moment when he'd first seen the beast. That evil kid had led him right into its clutches, delivering him to it like a bargain bucket of fried chicken. Panic had gripped him as every impulse screamed 'run', but his body refused to co-operate. And then it was too late. The thing had drenched him with spit, and he'd felt his legs go numb. After that, everything was a blank. Based on his current predicament, he guessed that the creature had hauled him back here to its lair, somewhere beneath the garden of Never Square.

Feeling the paralysing saliva beginning to wear off, he attempted to wiggle a finger. A tiny movement. It felt like a major victory, but unless he was going to dig his way out with his pinky it wasn't enough. He continued trying to work his hand free, but he needed options. His thoughts turned to Graham. With a bit of luck, he was already aware of Ryan's situation and was even now on his way to rescue him. Better yet, Graham had contacted the Doctor and she was on her way.

However, the hard truth was that he couldn't rely on either possibility. He had to figure something out by himself.

Slowly, his eyes were adjusting to his surroundings, and he could see more of what lay beyond the lantern's reach. The bones weren't all that was shining on the ground. He also caught the mirror glint of something metallic. It looked just like – and it seemed ridiculous even as the word popped into his head – a toaster. Just when he was roundly dismissing the idea as some kind of hallucination brought on by the poisonous saliva, he noticed another object next to it. He could have sworn it was a chrome kitchen tap.

There was a groan from the other side of the room, beyond the lamplight. Ryan stiffened, certain that it must be the creature. Then it happened again, and this time it sounded human.

'Hello?' Ryan ventured. 'Is someone there?'

There was a cough, then a weak voice said, 'Help . . . me.'

Ryan squinted past the glow of the lantern to discern the outline of another unfortunate prisoner encased in a mud straitjacket. There was someone else trapped down here.

'What's your name?' he asked.

'Tom,' the man replied in a whisper.

'I'm Ryan.'

Tom's thin voice gained strength, taking on a tone of outrage. 'Those people – they're monsters!'

'Not the monster I'd be worried about right now.'

Tom gave a desperate laugh.

'What's so funny?'

'I came to kill it. That's my job.'

'You're awful at your job.'

'It's some sort of mole, but I've never seen anything like it.'

Ryan could hear the shock in Tom's voice. It got him thinking. If the creature was basically a giant mole, maybe it had something in common with its regular-sized cousin? Something they could use. 'How were you going to kill it?'

'Spring-loaded traps. I know what you're thinking, but forget it. The most one of my traps would do to that thing is give it a sprained finger.' There was resignation in his voice.

Ryan wasn't giving up that easily. 'Come on, you're an expert. You're like a mole hitman. There must be something you can think of.'

There was a pause, as Tom racked his brains. 'Moles are fiercely territorial. If another one came into the run, they'd fight each other.'

'Great. So your solution to our man-eating-monster problem is another man-eating monster?'

'Sorry. Though, to be fair, it wasn't something I was expecting to deal with when I woke up this morning.'

'I bet the Doctor would know what to do.'

'Who's he?'

'She is . . .' Ryan caught himself before he said *a Time Lord from the planet Gallifrey*. Instead, he finished with, 'A very smart and resourceful friend.'

'Pity she isn't here,' Tom said.

'Wait!' A thought struck Ryan. 'She kind of is.'

By flexing his trapped fingers, he'd managed to scratch out a space around his hand. Now he used what leverage he had to claw through the mud to find his pocket. He dug furiously. After what felt like hours but was really only a matter of minutes, he had penetrated a few centimetres. He felt for the outline of the white cube. Nothing. Breaking out in a cold sweat, he wondered for a moment if he'd put it in the other pocket – but he was *positive* it had been this one. The pocket was empty. That meant he'd lost it. When the creature had lugged him from the tunnel to the lair, the cube must have fallen out.

Ryan felt the fight go out of him – almost. He rallied himself once more. There was still a chance the cube was here in the lair somewhere.

'Okay, Doctor,' he called out.

No reply.

One more try. 'Okay, Doctor!'

He held his breath.

A second later, a pinprick of light appeared in the darkness and the Doctor's voice sang out, 'Hello, Ryan. I'm listening.'

The tiny holographic image popped up as she spoke the welcoming words. Ryan knew it was a facsimile of her, but he had never been happier to see anyone in his life.

'What in the blue blazes is that?' said Tom.

There wasn't time to explain. 'Doctor, how do we get out of here?'

He crossed the fingers of his free hand and hoped that he'd get a sensible answer and not some random stuff about sponge cake. A wide red beam fanned out from the cube. Ryan guessed it was scanning the lair for information.

'You appear to be entombed in mud,' said the hologram. 'How would you describe the consistency?'

'It's kind of like dried clay. I'm in a pot, basically. How does that help, exactly?'

'Earth singer Mariah Carey can reach a pitch of over three thousand hertz,' replied the Doctor's hologram.

'Uh, I think that device of yours is broken,' said Tom.

Ryan had to agree. The erratic cube had gone off on another useless digression.

'However, what is required here is a very low frequency,' the hologram went on, 'such as you'd find among the *basso profundo* opera singers of the planet Oktavist IV. I am now accessing my database for a recording of their performance of *The Magic Fruit*, in which the heroine, Carmina, using only her cunning and a pan-dimensional pineapple, outwits the evil Count Visakov, only to discover in the final act that he is, in fact, her father from a parallel world, and in order to preserve her freedom she must throw herself from the tallest tower in the – You know what? Not important right now. Stick something in your ears. Here it comes.'

It began as a faint hum, deep and restless, like the distant grumbling of some fairy-tale giant.

The humming grew rapidly, reaching into every corner of the lair. Ryan felt an uncomfortable pressure building in his ears. Now it was a choir of giants. There was nothing he could do to block the relentless sound but, just as he was thinking it couldn't get any worse, he heard a crack, and then another. He was suddenly aware that he could feel his arms. The sound had split open his mud prison. It was like that trick with the singer who shatters the wine glass using just her voice to reach – what was it called? Resonant frequency, that was it.

With a grunt, Ryan pushed at the weakened mud case and a chunk fell away. Quickly, he dug himself out and saw that Tom had done the same. They met in the middle of the lair, astonished at their escape.

The humming stopped.

'And that's just the overture,' said the hologram.

'Thanks, Doctor,' said Ryan, sweeping up the cube. 'Now we need to get out of this sewer.'

'To unclog a blocked drain, the best thing to use is your trusty plunger,' said the hologram. 'If you haven't got one handy, try borrowing one from a Dalek.'

Ryan shoved the cube back in his pocket, muffling the rest of the useless advice.

Tom picked up the lantern and swung it about, searching for a way out. More of their prison took shape in the beam. Among the gnawed bones littering the ground were dozens of shiny objects, including the toaster and kitchen tap Ryan had spotted. Some items had been down here so long they'd lost their lustre, but many gleamed in the rare light. There were pieces of jewellery, coins, trophies, and enough chrome kitchen gadgets to stock a homewares department.

'I think your mole might be half magpie,' said Ryan. He froze in fear, startled by a face, then realised it was just his own reflection in a mirrored serving tray.

Tom swept the lantern towards the back of the lair, picking out an archway in the mud wall. 'Come on,' he said, already moving towards it.

'No, wait.' Ryan placed a hand on his arm, and they both heard the now-familiar scuttling. 'It's coming.'

There was another sound too this time, as if something heavy was being dragged along the ground.

Tom shook his head, appalled at this turn in their fortunes. He made a decision. 'I'll distract it. You make a run for the surface.'

As brave as the offer was, Ryan wasn't going to let Tom sacrifice himself. 'No way. We're getting out of here together.'

What would the Doctor do? She'd never let one of her friends give their life for hers. No, she'd come up with a last-gasp plan – which, based on Ryan's panicked breathing, was right about now.

'Can moles see?' he asked.

'Yes,' said Tom, 'but not very well. Why?'

Ryan peered into the darkness. At the last tick of the last second, it came to him.

22. Run!

Yaz ran for her life along the never-ending corridor. She had experienced fear before, but nothing – not even her recent adventures with the Doctor – could have prepared her for this. Nine-year-old TARDIS Ryan had made good on his promise to scare her out of her skin.

'They're all in here,' he had said, then proceeded to reel off a list of strange names. 'Autons, Ogrons, Daemons, Plasmatons, Cryons, Zygons . . .' The list continued, seemingly as endless as the corridor. 'Draconians, Osirians, Silurians, Sontarans . . .'

Ryan's measured voice possessed the power of an incantation, summoning fear from the shadows. Yaz sensed something cold and eyeless detach itself from a wall, and decided not to hang about.

The boy's words stalked her down the corridor. 'Kraals, Thals, the Fendahl, Haemovores, Tritovores . . .'

Yaz was being pursued, but by what exactly she couldn't be sure. Whenever she risked a backwards glance, her timing was just off and she failed to catch sight of it. Either the lighting was too dim to make out more than a blurry shape, or the thing would be round a corner and not quite in view. She wasn't about to wait for it to catch up.

It's not real, she tried to persuade herself. *It's just another construct.* But her rational brain was overwhelmed, swamped by primitive instinct. All she could do was run.

'Robots of Death, the K1 Robot, the Kandyman, L3 robots, White Robots, clockwork robots, Handbots, Illyria Seven robots, robot knights . . .'

It was coming for her. Slouching, slithering, marching.

'Ice Warriors, Sea Devils, War Machines, Time Zombies, Weeping Angels . . .'

As Ryan's voice droned on, something strange happened to the corridor. It began to alter its appearance. Sometimes it was dark and cavernous, other times bright and shiny. One second the walls were smooth and curved, the next they were stony and rough. Briefly, it was lit by guttering torches, then by powerful floodlights. Yaz would skid round the next corner to find herself ankle-deep in murky water, and a moment later be forced to pick her way through a series of criss-crossing laser tripwires.

And, always at her back, the sense that something was about to dig its claws into her.

'What scares you, Yaz?' Ryan had asked. 'There are fifteen hundred years' worth of fright in here. Every monster the Doctor has faced. Voord, Ood, Judoon, Mandrels, Argolins, Destroyers . . .'

She felt her heart beat faster, her throat tighten.

'Jagrafess, Reapers, Pyroviles, Silents . . .'

The walls of the corridor bulged with faces contorted in terror. Yaz stumbled and fell, one leg folding awkwardly beneath her.

'Snowmen, Whisper Men, Cybermen . . .'

It was coming for her. She could hear it, snorting, groaning, screeching.

'Extermi–'

Wait!

There was a door. At the end of the corridor. The first she'd seen since arriving in this purgatory. Maybe it led to another corridor, but it could be a way out. Either way, it was her only option. She picked herself up, wincing as she put weight on her left leg. She'd twisted her ankle. Ignoring the pain, Yaz limped for the door, her only thought to escape.

'Hurry,' said Ryan evenly. 'It's going to get you.'

She felt a *whoosh* of air as something clawed at her back and missed. The door flew open and she let out a scream as she tumbled through it.

Yaz had fallen right back into the TARDIS console room. She spun round to slam the door in the face of whatever pursued her, only to find that both had vanished – as had the pain in her ankle. There was no sign of Ryan, either.

The Doctor was here, though, feverishly working the TARDIS controls and too intent on her task to notice Yaz. The TARDIS lurched as if it was caught up in a storm, and Yaz grabbed the edge of the console to steady herself.

'Doctor,' she said, surprised at how feeble her voice sounded. Her experience in the corridor had left her shaken.

'Yaz! Good to have you back.' The Doctor waved away the smoke that was pouring from the damaged console. 'Sorry I couldn't help. Been a bit busy outrunning the Gardener warship.'

A map appeared on the wall of the TARDIS, displaying the path of the pursuit, using two dotted lines to mark the progress of each ship. So far it looked as if the warship had chased the crippled TARDIS through an asteroid field, round a black hole, and briefly into the upper atmosphere of a nearby planet. As Yaz watched, the Doctor heeled the TARDIS round a small moon, and the warship adjusted its course to follow. It stuck to its quarry like green on a leaf.

'Did you get the co-ordinates?' asked the Doctor.

Her heart sank as she was reminded of Mrs Knowles's unbelievably trite words. Useless. Completely and utterly –

Wait a minute.

Of course! That's why the TARDIS didn't move. It was already where it needed to be. 'No,' she replied. 'I have something even better.'

The Doctor glanced up briefly, her expression uncharacteristically puzzled.

'Remember the prophecy in the rose garden on Tellus IV? You said they'd got it wrong –

that the number thirteen referred to the vault, not to you. You were right. And you were also wrong.'

Yaz reached for the loop of string round the Doctor's neck, gently pulling on it until the object at the end of it popped above her collar.

'The key to Vault Thirteen,' said Yaz, dangling the TARDIS's key in front of her.

The Doctor peered at it for a moment, then a broad grin split her face. 'Result!'

Briefly, Yaz thought of the creators of the Galactic Seed Vault, aided by the Time Lords in hiding their keys across the universe. They could have picked anywhere and anywhen. It was neither chance nor fate that the latest key had ended up here. Yaz studied the Doctor, who was intently focused on coaxing more speed from the TARDIS. If Yaz wanted to keep the most precious item in the universe out of the wrong hands, she would have entrusted it to the Doctor too.

There was a dull thud, and the TARDIS shook from side to side. This knock felt different from the previous attacks.

'What was that?' asked Yaz.

'We're in range of their tractor-beam,' said the Doctor.

Yaz pictured a big green farm vehicle straining against a tow rope tethered to the TARDIS. The console room juddered, as the ship resisted the pull of the beam.

'Can you shake it off?'

'We're in a TARDIS, Yaz.' The Doctor's tone was haughty and dismissive. 'Even in one that's on the blink like this one, it's like racing a Formula One car against ... a patio.' She hovered a hand over a lever, looked up and grinned. 'Watch this!'

23. We Belong Together

Graham regained consciousness to find himself being dragged along an underground passage by the creature that had snatched him from the garden. He bumped along on his back, one leg stretched out before him, ankle clasped in the thing's dirty, sun-starved paw.

In the gloom, he could make out a pair of powerful hind legs and a sleek fur coat. He wrinkled his nose. The creature reeked. The sharp smell awakened the recent memory of the ritual, and angry thoughts flooded him as he recalled Delgado and the Never Square residents offering him up to this monster as a sacrifice. If he got out of this, he swore he'd extract his revenge – maybe trample over their precious flower beds. Right at that moment, though, payback seemed a long way off.

The creature adjusted its direction, and Graham felt himself swing round a bend. He saw something glint beneath the other front paw, tucked close to the creature's body. The espresso machine. For one horrible moment, he pictured the creature making itself a cappuccino and dunking him in it like a human biscotti. He had to escape before he became elevenses. But how? His one free leg scuffed along the ground. If he timed it right, a well-aimed kick might release him from its grip. But, even if by some miracle it dropped him, what then? He could run, but it was faster.

The creature swerved to avoid an obstruction. Graham glimpsed it as they swept past: a fat metal tube poking from the tunnel roof. It was riddled with rust and its blotchy surface was ringed with several angular fins, so that it appeared as if a space rocket had misjudged its landing. Graham didn't give it any further thought. There were probably loads of weird things buried down here.

Several turns later, he detected a faint light up ahead and felt the creature pick up the pace. Graham could sense its hunger to get to what he presumed must be its lair. His final destination. Desperately, he dug his fingers into the soil floor of the passage, trying to slow their progress, but his captor was too strong and he succeeded only in leaving two long furrows in the earth. Even though he knew it was futile, he kicked out, but the beast simply shrugged him off. All he had left were curses, but insults weren't going to have any effect on its animal brain. It was feeding time. The light grew brighter as they approached the lair. The creature scrabbled under a low archway and came to a dead stop.

There was another of the creatures in here, waiting.

Graham groaned in horror. He was dinner for *two*.

Then, to his astonishment, he felt the unyielding grip loosen. He was free – at least, he was for now.

The monster let out a squeal, flared its star-shaped nose and charged at its dinner companion. It covered the short distance in a matter of seconds and, running full tilt, smashed head first into the other creature. There was a bone-cracking crunch as the two met and then, to Graham's puzzlement, the other creature collapsed in a noisy tumble of shining pans and trays, chrome taps and polished kettles.

He now saw that the kitchen appliances had been carefully stacked against a wall to create a makeshift mirror. There was no second monster, only a reflection of the first.

The creature unsteadily took a step, then collapsed to the ground. The collision had knocked it out.

'I don't believe it,' said a man Graham didn't recognise, emerging from the shadows. 'It worked. Kid, you're a genius.'

The man was addressing a second figure, who Graham now saw was Ryan.

'Graham!' Ryan's face lit up.

Graham pulled his grandson into a hug. For a change, Ryan didn't resist.

'This is Tom,' Ryan said by way of introduction. 'He's a rubbish pest exterminator.'

'Time to go,' said Tom. 'That thing stunned itself, but it won't be out for long.'

'The key,' blurted Graham. 'It's here. Has to be.' He snatched the lantern from Tom and swung it over the mess of homewares.

'Key? What key?' asked Tom, watching bewildered as the other two scoured the space. Despite his pleading, it was clear they weren't going anywhere until they'd located it, so with great reluctance he joined in the search. Five minutes turned into ten, with no success.

'Please,' said Tom.

Graham was on his hands and knees among the bones. 'Not yet. Just a few more min–'

He'd spotted something poking out of the eye socket of a skull. A highly polished silver key.

With rising excitement, Graham darted a hand towards it, and just as he did so the mole creature's hind leg twitched. He felt his fingers close round the cool metal, and jumped up, making for the archway alongside the others.

Since both Ryan and Tom had been unconscious during their journey to the lair, it fell to Graham to lead the way back to the surface. Guided by the lantern, he did his best to retrace the creature's steps. He took the first couple of turns confidently, but the mole had carved out a maze beneath the garden. The task grew increasingly difficult.

He hesitated at an unfamiliar junction. 'This way,' he said striking off down the right-hand passage.

'You sure?' asked Ryan.

He wasn't, but then he noticed something halfway along the section of tunnel. 'Definitely. See that space rocket?' By the lamplight, he pointed out the object he'd noticed earlier.

'That's not a space rocket,' said Tom.

'Well, obviously.' Graham wasn't a complete idiot.

'But it *is* a rocket. A German one.'

Graham froze. 'It's a bomb?'

'A UXB,' muttered Ryan, remembering his conversation with Jonathan. 'Is it still dangerous?'

'Could be,' said Tom. 'Or it could be a dud. But, if it is live, it won't take much to set it off. I've heard stories. One touch of a spade, a good shove, even a harsh vibration and *kaboom*!'

'Shh!' hissed Ryan. 'D'you hear that?'

The other two instantly fell silent. As Graham listened, he registered the dreaded scuttling sound coming from the passage behind them and felt the blood drain from his face. 'Oh no.'

'Hurry!'

One by one, they edged past the bomb, each holding their breath as they ducked under the jutting device. As he passed it, Ryan had a thought. He reached into a pocket and drew out the Doctor's cube, then carefully wedged it into the mud roof of the tunnel as close to the bomb casing as he dared.

'Ryan,' Graham whispered urgently. 'What are you doing? Come on!'

Ryan held up a finger. He needed time. 'Okay, Doctor.'

'Hello, Ryan,' said the hologram. 'I'm listening.'

'Are there any people nearby?'

'Other than you three, I detect no human life signs in a seventy-eight-metre radius.'

'Okay. In thirty seconds, I want you to play some Mariah Carey.'

'We belong together,' said the Doctor.

'I know,' said Ryan sadly. 'But I can't take you with me.' He understood that she was only a hologram, but even so he felt bad leaving her here.

'No, Ryan. I mean the song. "We Belong Together". Okay?'

'Oh, yeah, right.' The scuttling was getting closer. He was running out of time. 'Thirty-second countdown, then full Mariah. Got it?'

'Got it, Ryan. Good luck. Thirty . . . twenty-nine . . .'

'Run!' Ryan yelled to the others.

The three men didn't look back. Ryan kept up the countdown in his head, as they bolted along the passage. When he reached twenty, he was sure he could feel the ground begin to slope up towards the surface. They were almost out of here. Then, as they rounded the next bend, they came to a dead end.

Fifteen seconds.

'I think I might've taken a wrong turn,' said Graham.

Ryan felt a waft of fresh air at his feet and looked down. 'I know where we are.' He pointed at a square hatch in the wall. They'd almost missed it in the darkness. He kicked it open, and the three of them squeezed through the gap, coming out in the air-raid shelter. 'Quickly, find something to cover the hole.'

Tom and Graham pushed the bench against it, as Ryan mouthed the final countdown.

'Three . . . two . . . one.'

He held his breath. He knew it was unlikely, but he was convinced that at that exact moment he heard Mariah Carey's powerful voice hit a bomb-trembling high note. A second later there was a dull *whump* from deep within the network of tunnels. The makeshift barrier of the bench was blown over in a cloud of dust and debris, and the corrugated-iron shelter shook like an angry giant was trying to tear it apart with his bare hands. The three men crouched on the floor, covering their heads with their arms as they waited for the effects of the explosion to subside.

After the initial detonation came a series of thuds, as if something was banging on the outside of the shelter's roof. Then silence.

When, after a cautious delay, the three of them ventured outside, it was to find the garden a smoking wreck. Lights had come on in all the surrounding townhouses, and the scene was illuminated by the glow. There was a large crater where the lawn had been, small fires had erupted across the flower beds, and two sides of the iron fence railings were completely flattened, opening the view up to the street. The thudding they'd heard was the sound of clods of earth raining down across Never Square. The devastation was total. However, it seemed the party had broken up following the end of the ritual, so there were no casualties. At least, no human ones. Livid chunks of the mole creature lay across what was left of the garden – in the herbaceous borders, and hanging off the branches of the well-tended trees. Ryan prodded a piece with his toe. It smelled even worse on the inside than it had on the outside.

The explosion had also thrown bones from the creature's lair to the surface. Graham contemplated the remains. The sacrificial victims sent to their doom by Delgado and his neighbours had finally made it back to the upper world. His thoughts were interrupted by the ring of a metal gate being thrown open. It was Delgado and the others. They poured into the garden, their faces displaying shock and dismay at the carnage.

Delgado caught sight of Graham, who gave him a cheery wave and a big smile.

'Why are you grinning at him?' asked Ryan.

'Just picturing the moment he and his cronies have to explain all of these human remains to the cops.'

From a nearby street came the wail of approaching sirens. The emergency services were on their way. They were not the only ones. Out of the corner of his eye, Graham noticed a flashing blue light beyond a section of the fallen fence railings.

'The police are here,' said Tom.

'That's not a patrol car,' said Graham, striding off across the garden, taking particular pleasure in treading through the flower beds. 'Stick that in your by-laws,' he muttered. 'Ryan?'

'Right behind you.' Ryan turned to a bewildered Tom. 'Uh ...' Leaving people without a proper goodbye or much in the way of an explanation was turning into a habit. In the end, he simply stuck out a hand and said, 'Nice to meet you. Good luck with your moles.' With that, he shot after Graham.

They emerged on to the street outside the garden to find the TARDIS waiting for them at the same corner where they'd been dropped off earlier that day. As they approached, the door glided open. They stepped inside.

'One slightly saliva-covered key,' said Graham, holding it up triumphantly. 'You have no idea what we went through to get it, but rest assured I plan to fill you in on every excruciating detail just as soon as I've had a long bath and a cup of –'

He froze at the sight of the frightening figure standing over the TARDIS's control console, bandolier of blooms strung across his chest, blaster clutched in his hand. A worm wriggled across one leafy cheek.

'Nightshade.'

24. The Crack of Doom

Nightshade surveyed the Time Lord and her sorry crew, lined up before him on the command bridge of – what had she called it? – the TARDIS.

He had captured the vessel with his tractor-beam and brought it aboard his flagship. At first, the Time Lord had refused him entry, so he'd threatened her with a dose of noughtweed. The remarkable weed was capable of eating through any material in the universe, and she evidently did not relish the thought of it taking hold of her TARDIS. She had opened the doors promptly and, faced with a boarding party of his finest shock troops, she and her companion had put up no further resistance.

After that, it was a simple matter to capture the other two. He wanted them all where he could see them. He would leave nothing to chance. Or to prophecy.

'What happened?' the earthling named Graham asked the others.

'We lost a race to a patio,' replied the young female.

The earthlings were of little importance, but the Time Lord was another matter. Hadn't the First Gardener herself allied with this Doctor's predecessors? And now, so many seasons later, Gardener and Time Lord were brought together again. The circularity pleased Nightshade. However, unlike his illustrious ancestor, he couldn't rely on this Time Lord to help him in his mission.

He had pursued her since Tellus IV, where, having missed the opportunity to stop her there, he had destroyed the Rose Garden of Eternity. If he was honest with himself, he had done so in a fit of pique, for its destruction had not laid his fears to rest. The prophecy in the flowers had not withered along with the blooms. The Doctor had remained a threat – until now. He had chased her round the moon of Tartarus, and through the Vordanian maelstrom. Now she was at his mercy, and he was not known for his merciful nature. He would dispense with her soon enough. For the moment, he relished the near-instantaneous travel afforded by her timeship, so he had to tolerate her existence a while longer. It was essential that he be present when Vault Thirteen fell, but only she could pilot the TARDIS.

'Doesn't say much, does he?' said the young male.

The Doctor shrugged. 'Once you've heard one villainous monologue, you've heard 'em all.'

Nightshade ignored their prattling, and reflected on his own journey. Of course, there had been setbacks along the way – failure and sacrifice and so much death – but they signified nothing when viewed in the long planting of the universe. And, like the rest of his kind, Nightshade held endless reserves of patience. However, even he felt the quickening of anticipation. After all these years, his time was coming.

'I still don't understand how he found the TARDIS,' said the young female.

There was a movement at the edge of the console room, and one of the Gardener troops returned from the TARDIS's interior. He held something in his gloved hands, but it was obscured in shadow.

'Tracking device,' said the Doctor. 'A plant.'

Clutched in the soldier's grasp they now saw the familiar begonia.

'Greetings, Gray-ham, Giver of Water.' Its leaves fluttered like contemptuous laughter.

Graham regarded his houseplant with confusion. 'You?'

'The gardening boot is on the other foot now, eh, my friend?'

'Who wears gardening boots?' Graham shook his head in sadness and disbelief. He gestured to Nightshade. 'What did he promise you, eh? A sunnier window? A bigger pot?'

'Perhaps this will teach you not to go off to Blackpool and forget to water your houseplants. You monster. You *killed* her.' The plant's voice caught. 'My succulent darling, Vera.'

Graham winced. He did remember managing to kill off several plants through neglect. Even the hardy aloe had withered under his care. But, still, that hardly merited selling out the entire universe to a cult of plant-mad aliens, did it?

'Enough.' When Nightshade finally spoke, they all heeded his word.

*

Vault Thirteen was not as they had left it. Snow fell silently through the air, coating the stone trees and covering the ground in a crisp white layer. It fell on the roof of the TARDIS. Yaz turned her face up and saw through the blizzard that a large section of the roof was gone. The noughtweed, which had penetrated the shield wall guarding the entrance, had worked its way into the very rock, weakening the structure until it had fallen in on itself. The vault was open to the frozen skies of Calufrax Major, and with its defences down the Doctor had been able to fly right into its heart.

The noxious weed was everywhere: coating the walls, entwined round the stone trees, sprouting from every crack. Smashed seed jars littered the snow, their contents exposed. Many were ruined, killed off by the freezing elements, but a few of the hardier super-fast germinators had sprung to life. Around the vault, green shoots poked out of the snow, and red and blue flowers bloomed in the unlikely surroundings. Some of the blooms snapped and gnashed, but even the Venusian gulpers were no match for the all-consuming noughtweed. It smothered everything in its path; writhing, multiplying, unstoppable. It had reached the wooden door and was working on making its way through the paralock, guzzling down aeons of time like water.

Gardener troops stood guard around the vault. The Attendant was their prisoner, every segment of its legs tightly bound by weaponised garden twine. Under Nightshade's wary eye, the Doctor and her companions were marched across the room.

'Before the end of the day, my noughtweed will open a door that has been locked for millennia,' he crowed. 'The Genesis Seed will be mine.'

'Why wait?' said the Doctor. 'Let me open it for you.' She dangled the TARDIS key in front of him.

Nightshade regarded the Doctor with deep suspicion. He had confiscated two of the vault keys, but hadn't known the identity of the third. Until now.

'Doctor!' hissed Yaz. 'What are you doing?'

'Trust me,' she said, and was immediately distracted by a gangling plant nearby. It had shot up, beanstalk-like, from its obliterated seed jar. Dozens of waxy pods dangled from its stems. 'Doppelpods,' she said delightedly, striking off towards it through the snow. 'Haven't tried these since I visited the Celestial Potting Sheds of Uzamox.' She plucked a pod

240

and popped it open to reveal half a dozen purple pea-like fruits inside. She tossed them into her mouth – then immediately spat them back out again. 'Forgot how disgusting they are,' she muttered.

'Uh, Doctor,' said Ryan. 'How about we save the universe first and snack after?'

'Give me the key,' commanded Nightshade, reaching for it.

The Doctor snatched it up and away from him. 'Okay, here's the deal,' she said. 'I'll open the door on the condition that you release my friends and the Attendant unharmed.' She cut off his objection. 'Sure, you could wait for your slithery friend to do its stuff, but what if the contents are damaged when the vault breaks? What if there's some fiendish ancient booby trap that's triggered by an unauthorised entry? What if it gives me time to think of a better plan?' She shrugged her shoulders. 'Why take the risk?'

Nightshade was silent as he considered the offer. He gave a solemn nod.

Yaz couldn't blame him. He didn't have to trust the Doctor, since he held all the cards. What did he have to lose?

'Onwards.' Pulling her coat round her, the Doctor crunched on through the snow and circled the pool, edging past the slippery noughtweed vines half submerged in the strange, time-frozen water like the tentacles of a colossal sea monster. As she moved past the Attendant, it lunged in fury, only prevented from reaching her by the firmness of its bonds.

Yaz had no doubt that the beetle was telepathically hurling insults into the Doctor's head.

'Don't do this,' Ryan pleaded.

Stepping carefully round the noughtweed, the Doctor waved her key over the door. A lock popped into existence.

'Quantum superposition,' she noted. 'Lock and key are linked on a subatomic level. Each is simultaneously there and not there. Very interest–' She caught Nightshade's impatient expression and offered up the TARDIS key.

He studied it for several seconds. 'No. You open it,' he said, handing over the other two keys.

'Suspicious fellow, aren't we?' she said. 'All right, then. Ryan? Graham?'

Ryan took the copper-coloured key they'd acquired on New Phaeton with its delicate engraving. Graham collected the polished silver key from the mole creature's lair, which in this light had a green hue and glistened like grass after a rainstorm. The Doctor gripped the TARDIS key. On the face of it an ordinary if tarnished Yale key, it was in reality a highly advanced piece of technology, with a plasmic shell incorporating a low-level perception filter, resistant to almost anything but prolonged exposure to lava, and designed to unlock the double-curtain trimonic barrier installed on the Type 40.

'Ready?' said the Doctor.

Yaz watched her friends, their keys poised to unlock the door. The first time they had visited Vault Thirteen, the Attendant had warned them that the Genesis Seed was the most dangerous in existence, a device of unimaginable power. Here they were, about to release it.

'Okay, people,' said the Doctor. 'The keys must be turned at precisely the same moment, or the door will not open.'

Ryan pushed his key into the first of the three locks that had appeared in the wooden door. Billions of years parted before it as easily as a curtain. Graham followed his example, and the Doctor slid the TARDIS key into the third lock.

'All right,' she said. 'On the count of three. One . . . t–'

'Wait!' Graham held up a hand.

'Oh, come on!' Ryan gasped. Adrenaline was coursing through his body, and his hand was shaking with the responsibility of the moment.

'Do we turn *on* three or *after* three?' Graham asked.

'It's always on. Who turns after?' The Doctor gave a tut. 'Let's try that again.' She paused. 'One . . . two . . . three!'

Ryan felt his key turn smoothly in the lock. He held his breath, waiting to discover if they had timed it correctly. He didn't have to wait long. With a series of clunks, the door swung open. Before them lay the inner vault, shrouded in darkness.

The Doctor drew herself up to her full height, her expression at once darker and more alien than the others had ever seen. She began to recite in a low voice.

'*I watched as he opened the sixth seal. There was a great earthquake. The sun turned black like sackcloth made of goat hair, the whole moon turned blood red, and the stars in the sky fell to earth, as figs drop from a fig tree when shaken by a strong wind.*'

A fearful silence settled over them.

Then the Doctor grinned. 'Who wants to go first?'

25. Forbidden Fruit

The inner vault was empty.

In his hurry to cross the threshold, Nightshade hadn't objected when the Doctor and her companions filed in behind him. A thin layer of dust coated the flagstone floor of what was a windowless chamber. Rough-hewn walls arched above them, shadowy alcoves built into either side. The only light came from the door through which they'd entered.

Yaz knew that the room had lain undisturbed for an unimaginably long time, yet she felt a strong presence, as if the last occupant had just stepped out.

'Where is it?' Nightshade dropped to the floor, and began to frantically scour the dust-laden surface.

'Maybe this is an antechamber,' said Graham. 'And, y'know, the Chamber of Secrets or whatever is next door. Look for one of those candlestick things attached to a wall.'

'You mean a wall sconce?' said the Doctor.

'Yeah.'

'Why?'

'So we can pull it. That's what you do.' He stepped further into the room. 'You pull on the wall sconce and a secret passage op–'

'Don't move!' commanded the Doctor, flinging out a hand to restrain him.

Graham froze, one foot outstretched, while the Doctor knelt down and gently drew a circle in the dust. At the centre of it was a single, tiny seed.

Taking it gently between index finger and thumb, she lifted it into the light.

Nightshade scrabbled to her side, then stopped. He gazed at the seed, at first too stunned to react.

Yaz knew she was meant to feel awestruck, but the reality was that it just looked like a completely average seed. 'Is that it?'

The Doctor turned the seed over in her fingers, inspecting it from every angle as if that might reveal its secrets. 'Apple, if I'm not mistaken.'

'The Genesis Seed,' breathed Nightshade. 'You hold in your hand the very beginning of the universe. A seed of the tree from which everything around us grew. And with it we shall begin again.'

Slowly, the truth began to dawn on the Doctor's companions.

'The Genesis Seed comes from an *apple* tree?' said Yaz.

'Are you saying . . . Is this . . . the Tree of . . . N-n-n-no,' Ryan stuttered.

Graham shook his head in wonder. 'I don't Adam and Eve it.'

'If you're asking me if this is a seed from the Tree of Knowledge in the Garden of Eden,' said the Doctor. 'Then the answer is . . . could be. How did it get here? Funny thing about beginnings. Even civilisations at opposite ends of the universe often tell the same story about where they came from. That's the power of stories for you.'

'The soil must be turned,' Nightshade intoned.

'Chanting ominous phrases is all very well.' The Doctor sighed. 'But what, exactly, are we talking about here? How does this tiny little seed bring about the end of everything? Hmm? Entropy wave that causes universal heat death? Reality bomb? Dimensional transference

247

triggered by a black-light explosion? Every star exploding at every point in history? Been there, done that, bought the T-shirt.' She turned to her companions. 'There is actually a T-shirt commemorating my epic saves. Got it in the gift shop on the planet Shada. Terrible place. Designed so that once you're in you can never find your way out.'

'It is time for this universe to be dug over in preparation for the next,' said Nightshade. 'The Genesis Seed is not unlike noughtweed, but it works on an unimaginably larger scale.'

The Doctor stood at the edge of one of the dark alcoves. The seed lay on her palm, an insignificant speck no bigger than a single teardrop. 'Try me. I have a big imagination.'

Nightshade gazed at the seed with the flame-bright eyes of a true believer. 'Soon after germination begins, a hole will form in the space around the seed. A black hole of unfathomable magnitude. Roots will spring forth from the abyss, reaching out across the event horizon, winding endlessly through the universe, overrunning everything in their path, tearing apart the fabric of space. All this will happen in the first few seconds after germination. Then galaxies, solar systems, individual life forms will break free from their gravitational bonds and be sucked down into the black hole. This universe, along with everything in it, will be planted in the deepest reaches. The soil will close overhead and the screams of the dying will be as birdsong to the dawn of the new universe that will arise from the remnants of the old. Life is unimportant. All are fertiliser in the end.'

The shocked silence that followed was broken by a commotion from outside: shouts and the blast of weapon fire. A moment later, the Attendant whirled into the inner vault and, its mandibles snapping like scissors, tackled Nightshade to the floor. The other Gardeners were not far behind. They jumped on to the beetle, straining to pull it off their leader.

In the ensuing scuffle, a Gardener warrior grabbed Graham, who yelled, 'Get off me, you overgrown privet hedge!'

Nightshade got to his feet, seemingly unruffled by the assault. He faced the Doctor and stuck out a hand. 'It is time.'

The Doctor hesitated, then surrendered the seed.

'No! What have you done?' The Attendant levelled its telepathic wrath with such force that it rang in every head.

From somewhere deep within himself, Graham summoned the strength to shake off his captor.

Desperate to help save the day, he rushed headlong at Nightshade, but covered only a few steps before he was intercepted. He glimpsed the butt of a black-ash blaster descending, then a light exploded in his head, and that was the last he knew.

'Graham!'

Ryan and Yaz ran to help, but were prevented from reaching him by a wall of Gardeners. As they were forced away from their friend, Yaz struggled to comprehend the Doctor's actions. Why had she given up the seed so easily? Surely she didn't trust Nightshade to keep his end of the deal? She felt the prod of a weapon in her back, and followed the Attendant, who was putting up a furious fight, outside. In the chaos, she saw that the Doctor had somehow got ahead of her and was now standing silently behind Ryan.

As Yaz emerged from the inner vault, the ground shook and a loosened boulder crashed into the pool. The stone trees were splintering under the crushing pressure of the noughtweed. The shield wall flickered as it lost power. Vault Thirteen was in its death throes.

From above came the roar of engines. Yaz looked up to see one of the scoop-shaped craft that had devastated Tellus IV descend through the blizzard, its hot engines bright against the leaden sky. It manoeuvred neatly through the open roof, then levelled off. The landing gear unfolded, and the craft touched down, settling in a deep drift of snow.

'Take the saplings aboard,' Nightshade commanded. Gardener warriors grabbed Ryan and Yaz, and began hauling them towards the ship. 'It is fitting that two of your young will bear witness to the moment of new growth.'

'Hey!' Yaz wrestled with her captors. 'He is not Adam, and I am definitely not Eve.'

'Doctor, do something!' yelled Ryan.

The Doctor didn't reply, just stood at the edge of the pool, watching in silence. Her expression was one that Yaz had never seen before: glassy, empty. *Defeated*. Had she really given up?

'And you, Time Lord,' said Nightshade. 'You stand for the old universe. Console yourself with the knowledge that your young companions will share the moment of my triumph, but you –' he raised a hand – 'have pruned my plans once too often.'

From her position halfway up the ramp, Yaz couldn't see what Nightshade was holding, but a moment later there was a fierce sizzling noise and the bright pulse of weapon fire. The Doctor fell.

'No!' screamed Yaz.

Beside her, Ryan let out a cry and sank to his knees.

A triumphant Nightshade stood over the Doctor's body. She lay in the snow as flakes continued to fall on her. Through her numbing fear, Yaz knew that she had seen this before. The vision she'd had when she was inside the TARDIS. It had come true.

The Doctor was dead.

26. An Apple a Day

The clunk of the closing hangar-bay doors signalled that Nightshade's shuttle had successfully returned to his command ship in orbit round Calufrax Major. As he headed to the bridge, he gave the order to plot a course to their next – and final – destination.

He felt no remorse for his actions on the planet below. All things must die. That was the way of the universe, and even the universe must obey its own laws. He was merely the agent of that change.

There was a buzz on the bridge. With the Time Lord dead, the prophecy of the Rose Garden of Eternity had lost its hold over the

253

crew. They sensed victory and the end of a mission set in motion millions of years ago. Nightshade took his place at his command station, setting down roots in the floor to anchor himself for the imminent acceleration, and opened his gnarled palm. The dormant Genesis Seed lay there. Unique. But, in some ways, not so different from any other.

He glanced up, as the Time Lord's young companions were marched on to the bridge. They posed no threat to him now, and had spent the duration of the journey in the shuttle clinging to one another in dismal silence. All that remained in them was a spark of anger, and they could do nothing with that other than to glower at him through eyes red with tears. Nightshade felt no impulse to console them or to justify his actions. In his anticipation of the end, he felt himself bathed with unexpected feelings of generosity. He wondered if his crew could see it upon him, shining like spring blossom.

'Navigator, give me a visual on our target.'

At his command, the crew member brushed a finger across a tightly budded flower, which opened, iris-like, at his touch. Like most of the systems aboard the Gardener ship, it was grown rather than built. A second later, the central screen was filled with an intense light. Powerful filters engaged, struggling to dim the image and protect the delicate sensors. Nightshade had to raise a hand to shield his eyes against the brightness. Yaz and Ryan did likewise, turning their heads away.

'What is that?' asked Yaz.

Nightshade answered the question with one of his own. 'What do you know about germination?'

Ryan huffed. 'Uh, I know that I am not about to listen to some boring lecture from a maniac who just murdered my friend.'

Nightshade ignored the boy. 'Most seeds require some combination of water, oxygen, darkness, light and heat in order to trigger the process that ultimately leads to them becoming fully grown. In the case of the Genesis Seed, it requires light and heat.'

Yaz had listened to his explanation in Vault Thirteen, and yet still couldn't comprehend how something as tiny and insignificant as an apple seed could bring about the destruction of the universe. But the Doctor hadn't contradicted Nightshade's firmly held belief, which meant it was true. The end was coming. The end of everything and everyone she knew and loved. It had already begun with the Doctor. If Nightshade got his way, the rest would soon follow.

'Time to destination?' he asked his navigator.

The crew member consulted the downy head of a dandelion clock. One quarter of the seeds had already flown. 'Fifty clocks until target.'

The buzz on the bridge intensified. Nightshade extended a hand, and a fat bumblebee – the source of the sound – settled on the end of one green finger. 'Unlike any other, the Genesis Seed requires a significant fusion reaction to trigger germination,' the Gardener said.

'Fusion?' said Yaz, aware of her heart beating faster.

The filters had finally dulled the blinding glare enough to make their destination visible on the main screen. She slipped her hand into Ryan's.

They were heading directly into Calufrax Major's sun.

Graham staggered out of the inner vault and collapsed to his knees, shivering in the cold air. His vision remained blurry, which he put down to his half-closed left eye. The result of a blaster butt to the face, from what he could dimly remember. The vault was empty. The Gardeners had left, and there was no sign of anyone else. Maybe the blow had left him unconscious for longer than he'd thought.

It was then that he spotted the TARDIS. He'd almost missed it, so completely did the noughtweed cover its exterior. A plague of curling tendrils had turned the familiar blue to a vile green. The door was ajar, which was one good thing. It meant the Doctor wasn't far away.

Graham looked about for her in the worsening blizzard, squinting through the driving snow until his one good eye came to rest on a dark shape lying on the ground. A terrible premonition gripped him, and he hurried over. As he drew closer, he saw that it was a figure, then realised with horror that it was the Doctor.

She wasn't moving.

Glassy eyes stared out of skin like paper. Gently, he reached out a hand to stroke her cold cheek. To his horror, as his fingers touched her skin, her face collapsed into dust. Shocked, he scrabbled away, only to see the rest of her body disintegrate and turn into the same fine ash, which was carried away on the wind.

'Graham, that is some shiner you've got there.'

He spun round at the sound of the voice.

It was her. The Doctor. Standing there alive and well.

He had never been happier to see anyone. Holding back a great sob of relief he gestured towards what he had assumed to be her remains.

'Doppelpod,' she explained. 'The plant mimics predators as a defensive measure. I figured a double might come in useful. The Attendant and I did a bit of private telepathic planning. The Attendant provided the distraction, and I carried out the switch. I've been hiding in one of those convenient shadowy alcoves.' She gestured with a thumb over her shoulder. 'You could say I was the other secret in Vault Thirteen.'

There was a great blast from above, and a downdraught blew the snow into a whirling vortex. Graham looked up through the gaping hole in the roof to make out the glow of engines. Some kind of craft was leaving the planet.

'What was that?'

'The Attendant,' said the Doctor. 'I'll explain later.'

Another earthquake shook the vault, stronger than the last one.

'Time we were off,' the Doctor said, striding towards the TARDIS.

Graham followed her inside. The noughtweed had penetrated the TARDIS too, tearing through the interior in the same way that it had overwhelmed the Galactic Seed Vault. Weeds clogged the console, carpeting the controls.

Struggling to reach the controls past the tangle of vines, the Doctor somehow managed to set the ship in motion. As it dematerialised, she activated the main scanner and it displayed the exterior of the Galactic Seed Vault. As the TARDIS sped away, Graham realised that they were watching the vault's last moments.

The great edifice that had withstood all the time in the universe buckled and fell.

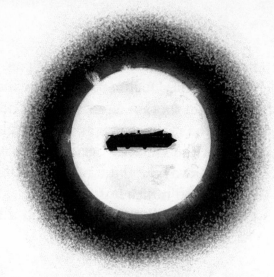

27. Plants Within Plants

Yaz and Ryan were locked up several decks below the bridge on the Gardener ship, in cells hurriedly prepared for them. Nightshade had intended to let them experience the sunstrike at his side. However, Ryan'd had other ideas.

'Yes, but did you have to hit him over the head with it?' Yaz asked.

They were in separate cells, divided from one another by a dense green wall of hedge. A narrow slit gave them a limited view of the corridor outside.

'He was asking for it,' said Ryan.

'I know, but a fire extinguisher?'

'I thought it was a log.'

Secretly, she was proud of him for standing up to Nightshade. Not that she'd tell him that. Then it struck her that she may never get another chance. What was she waiting for? Through the hedge, she could just make him out, exploring the inside of his cell. He was trying to figure a way out of here. They may have been heading straight into a sun and moments away from the end of the universe, but he hadn't given up.

Neither had she. On the march from the bridge to the prison deck, she had tried to take in as many details about the ship's layout and technology as she could, hoping to use any knowledge she could glean in a future escape attempt. From what she had observed, the ship was like a massive dugout canoe hollowed from a tree trunk that was capable of interstellar travel. She glanced into the upper corner of her cell, where a large red flower turned to follow her movements as she paced the floor. A security camera.

There was a groan from the adjacent cell, as Ryan vented his frustration. He punched a fist at the thorn-filled door, which accomplished nothing other than earning him a series of painful scratches across his knuckles.

Yaz took deep breaths and tried to still her rising panic. It didn't help. They were trapped and heading for the end of the universe. As she exhaled slowly for the third time, the breath caught in her throat, interrupted by the wail of an alarm. Outside her cell, she glimpsed a couple of guards dashing past, leaving their posts. Presumably called away to deal with something more urgent.

'What do you think that's about?' she said, trying to peer along the corridor, but unable to find an angle through the viewing slit.

'Don't know,' said Ryan. 'But they left in quite a hurry.'

There was a sound from just outside, and a moment later a face appeared in the narrow window.

'Graham!' Yaz pushed her face up to his, her expression of delight giving way to a wince. 'That is some shiner.'

From the adjacent cell, Ryan called out, 'Get us out of here! The ship's going to crash into the sun. We have to get the Genesis Seed before it hits.'

'Don't worry,' said Graham. 'The Doctor has everything under control.'

Ryan frowned in confusion. 'The Doctor? Our Doctor?'

'The one and only,' said Graham.

'She's alive?' Yaz wanted to scream with happiness. They were not out of the game yet.

The lights on the prison deck flickered.

'What was that?' said Yaz.

'Power surge?' suggested Ryan, certain that it was too minor to be of any significance.

'That, my friends,' said Graham, 'was our way out.'

Even with its advanced cooling systems, the temperature aboard the Gardener ship had climbed quickly as it approached the sun. But it was not the sun that had caused this latest spike in Nightshade's temperature. He studied his monitor in fury. Moments ago, the blue box had appeared in the hangar bay. The Time Lord was dead by his hand, but this was a worrying development. The prophecy of the rose garden flowered again in his mind.

He stabbed at a communicator. 'Prepare an assault team and meet me outside the hangar.' He would deal with this himself.

'Sir, I am detecting a ship trailing us. It appears to have originated from the Galactic Seed Vault.' A light began to blink on the weapons operator's console. 'A secondary object has detached from it and is bearing towards our position.'

'A counter-attack?'

'No weapon signature detected,' she replied, turning to her equipment array to study the incoming object. 'It appears to be one of the vault's seed-collecting drones.'

Nightshade flinched. It could be a weapon containing any number of lethal seeds. 'Scan for biologicals.'

There was a pause as the operator carried out his request. 'Nothing, sir. It's unarmed.'

Nightshade allowed himself to relax. No more than a futile gesture, then. A stone hurled into the sky to ward off the night. However, even though it was highly unlikely that a drone with its limited capabilities could penetrate their shields, now was not the time to take chances.

'Target the drone,' he commanded. 'Incinerate it.'

At another console, the weapons operator acknowledged the command and bent to her task. The object was already too close to the ship to engage it safely with missiles, so instead she activated the close-combat plasmas. These weapons weren't designed to bring down a target as small as the drone, so when the computers achieved a partial lock she took the shot. The first two salvos fired in quick succession. Both missed, and before she had a chance to launch a third the drone flew into the ship's shields and disintegrated on impact. The lights on the bridge flickered.

'Damage report,' demanded Nightshade.

'Negative,' came the reply. 'The drone was completely destroyed.'

If this was part of some devious Time Lord trick, he had dealt with it successfully, just as he had destroyed the Doctor herself. He hauled himself out of his chair and set off across the bridge. He had only got halfway when the door swished open and in she strolled.

She fanned herself with a large palm leaf. 'Is it hot in here, or is it me?'

'I killed you,' said Nightshade, in the face of the contradiction.

'Paul Daniels,' said the Doctor. 'Wonderful close-up magician. Taught me a lot about misdirection. You're going to like this. Not a lot.' She held out her free hand, which was clenched into a fist, then slowly opened it palm facing up.

On it lay an apple seed.

'No, not the Genesis Seed,' she said. 'But neither is yours.'

'You lie!'

She shrugged her shoulders. 'Remember when I persuaded you to let me open the door to the inner vault? That was so I could get close enough to the real seed to make the switch. Yours is an apple seed, all right, but it's one I picked up on

Tellus IV. At a picnic.' She closed her palm and blew on her fist. When she opened it again, the seed had vanished. 'And *that's* magic!'

A murmur of unease rippled through the crew. Could the Time Lord be telling the truth? Were they heading into oblivion for nothing? Nightshade stared at the seed in his hand. A question crossed his mind like a petal in the wind.

'No,' he said. 'I will not believe it.' His fingers closed over the seed again, and he clutched it tightly. But he sensed the misgivings among his crew, and he knew he had to quash their doubt before it spiralled into a mutiny. There was only one way. With his other hand, he drew his weapon, aimed and fired at the Doctor.

Nothing.

He tried again, with the same result. The blaster seemed to be malfunctioning.

'All your personal weapons are linked to the ship's systems for increased targeting accuracy. Isn't that so?' asked the Doctor.

It was true. The link gave them an edge in close combat.

'As of thirty seconds ago, your ship and its associated systems fell under its control.' The Doctor gestured with the palm leaf to the very centre of the bridge. 'Curatrix,' she said to the holographic figure standing there, 'how was your trip?'

The Galactic Seed Vault's AI consulted its clipboard before answering. 'Following your discussion with the Attendant, the seed-collecting drone carrying my consciousness launched at a velocity of one thousand eight hundred miles per hour, then collided eight point six seconds later with this vessel's shields, resulting in the drone's total physical destruction. It took me point zero three seconds to upload myself through the electrical barrier into the ship's systems.' The Curatrix made a tick on its clipboard. 'It is good to see you again, Doctor.'

28. Sunset

Fully operational, the Curatrix was an AI of staggering power and authority. The noughtweed had weakened it substantially, but with a boost from the Doctor it had regained most of its functionality. It therefore took mere milliseconds for the Curatrix to bring the Gardener warship's systems to its knees. The central processing unit succumbed with a whimper, surrendering its secrets and codes. In the cells, the flower cameras wilted, the hedges withered, and the way out was clear.

Ryan and Yaz were free.

Graham quickly led them to the nearest lift, as per the Doctor's plan. More alarms sounded at the escape attempt, triggering a security response. Guards converged on the prison deck only to be tripped up by the Curatrix-controlled systems. Doors opened, then swiftly closed behind the security teams, shutting them in. Artificial gravity was switched off in selected corridors, sending them floating into walls. Lifts carrying reinforcements came stuttering to a stop between floors, trapping the occupants. The Curatrix caused chaos for the Gardeners, while creating a clear escape corridor for the Doctor's companions.

'Fifteen clocks until sunstrike,' announced the helmsman over the ship-wide communication system.

Graham and the others hurried into the last working lift. The doors slid shut, and it jolted into motion. The hangar bay was five decks below them, and they reached it in less than a minute. The TARDIS was waiting, and Graham had the key.

When they got inside, Yaz froze at the sight of the console room. There was noughtweed all over the place, invading every surface, every system.

'The Doc says the TARDIS is going nowhere unless we can remove it,' said Graham.

Yaz swallowed hard. The Galactic Seed Vault hadn't been able to resist the weed, so how could the TARDIS?

From outside in the hangar bay, the voice echoed again. 'Fourteen clocks until sunstrike.'

Time wasn't running out. It was riding a roller coaster with its arms in the air, going, 'Aghhhhh!'

Graham looked to Yaz. 'She said you'd know what to do.'

'Do what?' asked Ryan desperately. 'What did the Doctor mean?'

Yaz understood, but there wasn't much time. Locating the dowsing rod half buried beneath the vines, she prised it from the console and repeated the steps she'd seen the Doctor perform. She clasped the glowing blue needle.

'Wish me lu–'

'I regret that I am no longer able to redirect the ship, Doctor. We are caught in the sun's gravitational pull.' An expression of concern slid across the Curatrix's face. 'Brace for solar flare!'

A moment later, the bridge shook with the force of the energy burst. The sun spat a cloud of electrons, ions and electromagnetic waves, which tore through the vessel's shields. An explosion ripped apart the weapons console, sending the operator flying across the bridge. She slumped against the bulkhead.

The Doctor ran to her side, inspecting the injured Gardener. 'She needs medical attention.'

'The solar flare has compromised all the ship's systems, including life support,' said the Curatrix. 'I am attempting to divert power from the main drive.'

The Doctor looked around at the rest of the crew. 'There's room for everyone aboard the TARDIS. We have to get you all off this ship. Now!'

The ship lurched again. 'Hull breaches on decks five through eight,' announced the Curatrix.

That was enough for the crew. Panicked by the deteriorating situation, the Gardeners began to scramble for the exits, picking up their fallen colleague as they fled.

'No!' yelled Nightshade. 'Remain at your posts. I order you to –'

Another explosion rocked the bridge. Splinters from a wooden control panel sheared off and spun through the air at high velocity, piercing his side. He let out a cry and stumbled, his legs going out from under him like two great trees being felled. Gardener blood, it turned out, was red too.

Yaz was somewhere else.

Not a corridor this time, but a street in an ordinary-looking town that seemed at once familiar and alien. No protective dome, no weird robots, no menacing monsters. Just two rows of cosy terraced houses, chimneys drawing smoke into the blue of an evening sky. Mingled with the tang of burning coal was the comforting smell of hot dinners. The only disconcerting aspect about the scene was that the street was empty. Not a soul. Not even a barking dog.

It was another construct, a scenario created by the TARDIS. Yaz didn't have time for any more games. If all went to plan, the Doctor and the others would be returning any minute. The timeship had to be back in action and ready to leave, or everything they'd achieved would be in vain.

'Come on,' Yaz muttered. 'Give me a clue here.'

From somewhere in the distance came the sound of music. A wild, looping tune full of swoops and howls. Its cosmic rhythm got under her skin, sending a shiver through her body. She determined that it was coming from the other end of the street, and hurried along the pavement, searching for the source, sure that when she found it she would be where she needed to be. Following the trail of musical notes, she swung past the gates of a school, noting the name on a plaque at the entrance: COAL HILL. The music led her on down a side street, and soon she found herself outside a pair of large wooden doors. Printed across them was the name of a business and its address: I.M. FOREMAN, SCRAP MERCHANT. 76 TOTTER'S LANE.

There was a gap between the doors big enough for her to squeeze through. On the other side was a junkyard heaped with piles of broken furniture, rusting washing machines and other assorted items no longer wanted by their owners. But Yaz noticed none of these. She was staring into a corner, where a blue police box stood under the glow of a street light.

The door banged open and the music swelled.

Small fires had erupted across the bridge of the Gardener ship, and the air was thick with smoke and the *whoosh* of automatic sprinklers. Nightshade lay crumpled on the floor next to his command chair, his bushy head resting on the Doctor's knees.

The holographic avatar of the Curatrix stood a little way off, observing the two of them. Even with all its processing power and aeons of deep learning, the AI could not understand why the Doctor remained by the side of a being who had tried to kill her not once, but twice, and who had tried to wipe out all life in the universe. The Curatrix noted that the leaves that covered Nightshade's face had already begun to curl and turn brown. Diverting a fraction of its resources from the task of keeping the ship in one piece, the Curatrix assessed the injury caused to him by the flying debris. It judged it to be fatal.

'You look like you've been dragged through a hedge backwards,' said the Doctor. 'Sorry. Been waiting ages to use that one.'

Nightshade struggled to speak. 'My people possess eternal patience, and yet even that is not enough to withstand your endless irritation.' He groaned and squeezed his eyes shut, as pain wracked his body.

'You don't really want to replace this universe,' said the Doctor. 'I mean, have you seen it? The Hanging Gardens of Babylon V. The Robotanical Gardens on Aether. Mrs Carol Carsley's bog garden in Dorset, England.'

Nightshade looked up at her through dimming eyes.

'Sure, this universe may be old,' the Doctor said, meeting his gaze, 'but it's still growing.'

Despite the automatic suppressant system, the flames had spread to the bulkhead and were raging out of control. However, the fire was of secondary concern. The Curatrix monitored the heat shield, which was the only thing keeping the ship from being incinerated by its proximity to the sun. As the AI attempted to squeeze a little more energy out of the engines to direct to the shield, it was distantly aware of another reading.

'Most Gardeners are content to bend their heads and tend the earth,' Nightshade said, wheezing with the effort. 'But I chose to get off my knees and look up.'

The Curatrix observed that his gaze was fixed and empty. 'His life has been extinguished,' it said.

'I know,' said the Doctor, gently laying his head on the floor. She took his hand and carefully prised open his fingers. The apple seed lay in a groove of his palm.

The Curatrix noted the subtle movement of the Doctor's facial muscles. 'That is an expression of relief. Why would you use that now, unless –' the Curatrix's eyes widened in realisation – 'that *is* the Genesis Seed.'

The Doctor reached into her pocket and pulled out Yaz's thermos flask. She popped the seed inside the flask, and screwed the top back on firmly.

'Course it is. What do you think I am – a magician?' She glanced up at what was left of the navigation console. The dandelion swayed amid the wreckage. 'Two clocks,' she said. 'Run!'

29. What Would
Werelock Do?

Yaz found nine-year-old Ryan tucked up in bed, shivering beneath a duvet patterned with childish illustrations of the TARDIS. It was just the sort of bedroom a sick nine-year-old would need, helpfully provided by the TARDIS. The boy lifted his head from his pillow and Yaz saw that his skin was pale, his nose red and swollen. He gave a hacking cough and lay down again. Beside him on the floor, a wastepaper basket brimmed with crumpled tissues. He reached an unsteady hand for another from a box and blew his nose loudly.

'I'm sick,' he groaned. 'Go away.'

'I'm here to help you get better.'

He laughed shortly. 'Know a lot about the TARDIS drive, do you? Transpower system? Dynamorphic generators? Ringing any Cloister Bells? When was the last time you used Zyton-Seven to transfer the Eye of Harmony's energy into orbital artron energy, eh?' He turned away from her and drew his legs up under the duvet.

Yaz sighed. This was going to be tougher than she'd hoped. She needed to find a different approach, and fast.

At the end of the bed sat a TV, an ancient, boxy thing with a tiny screen, its plastic casing designed to imitate natural wood. It stood on four equally fake wooden legs. There were two small buttons and two chunky dials set into the front for turning it on, adjusting the volume and selecting the channels. On the grainy screen, a programme was playing with the sound turned down – some kids' adventure series, by the look of it.

'What are you watching?' she asked.

'*Werelock Holmes*,' said Ryan without raising his head. 'By day he's an ordinary primary-school teacher, but once a month, during the full moon, he turns into a detective with wolf-based crime-fighting skills.'

It was the first time he'd shown any enthusiasm since she'd arrived, so Yaz decided to press on with this line. 'Sounds great.'

Ryan sat up, growing more animated by the second. 'It's a reboot of the classic series. Though not as family friendly as the original. To be honest, the stories are unnecessarily complex. But Werelock's still a great character, even after all these years. He's smart, brave, funny, never gives up.'

Yaz had an idea. 'So WWWD?'

'Huh?'

'What would Werelock do? How would he defeat the noughtweed and get back to full strength?'

'That's easy,' said Ryan, warming to the scenario. 'He'd transform himself. As soon as he changes from an ordinary person into a super-strong werewolf, nothing can harm him. Except silver bullets, obviously. But the change would do it.'

Yaz thought for a moment. That gave her an idea. 'Couldn't the TARDIS do the same? Change, I mean. Isn't it able to alter its form?'

'The chameleon circuit is . . . singular.'

'But it's possible?'

Ryan sat up. 'A massive blast of artron energy may theoretically reset the circuits. But it wouldn't be permanent.'

'Wouldn't have to be. Just enough to shake off this nasty cold.' She tore out a tissue and offered it to him. 'What do you say?'

The main hangar bay teemed with a forest of Gardener crew members, all desperately trying to escape immolation by the sun of Calufrax Major. Their own fanaticism and the will of Nightshade had brought them here, but with their cause in question and their leader gone their zeal had withered like autumn leaves. The remnants of Nightshade's personal guard attempted to keep order, but even the Grave Diggers lacked conviction in the face of what promised to be a fiery end. A few misguided souls had already departed in the handful of escape shuttles, sealing their own fates as the straining ships' engines blew themselves up vainly attempting to avoid being pulled into the sun.

The Doctor and Graham arrived in the hangar and surveyed the chaos.

'We can take everyone in the TARDIS, right?' said Graham.

'Space is not the problem,' said the Doctor, motioning to the noughtweed writhing round the police box, seemingly attempting to consume it like some gigantic prehistoric snake. 'Let's hope Yaz figured out a way to get rid of that stuff.'

'But you have a Plan B?' Graham asked nervously. 'In case she didn't?'

'Well . . .' The Doctor concentrated. 'We could try reversing the polarity of the neutron flow. That usually works.'

The blue light on top of the TARDIS flashed, as it began its dematerialisation sequence. The hangar bay fell silent, as the wheezing and groaning grew in volume.

'They're leaving,' said Graham in alarm. 'Without us.'

'Not so fast. Look.'

The TARDIS faded in and out of existence, and just when it seemed finally to have vanished, it rematerialised. But not in its usual form.

The TARDIS had become a tree.

Ancient and monumental, the gnarled trunk was at least three metres across and its leafy crown brushed the roof of the bay. Heavy branches reached out over the vast hangar, dripping with improbably blue fruit. The Gardeners bowed before the majestic sentinel, which towered over them with a regal air.

'A celestial mulberry,' said the Doctor. 'Not only rare and beautiful, but famously resistant to disease.'

With a shiver of leaves, the tree faded away again, and in its place sat once more the familiar blue police box. So startled was Graham by the transformation that it took him a moment before he realised that the noughtweed had gone.

30. Always Remember to Back Up

A dark speck moved across the face of the sun, as insignificant as a seed searching for the light. And then it was gone, consumed in an inferno of ionised helium, internal convective motion and hot plasma. When it came, it was not the end of the universe but a far smaller end.

The Doctor and her companions observed the final moments of the abandoned Gardener warship from the TARDIS, hovering in space safely protected from the sun's blistering energy behind freshly restored defensive systems. The

TARDIS's transformation had shrugged off the noughtweed with a sullen tut, like an ungrateful teen presented with the wrong brand of mobile phone by a clueless parent.

By the time the Doctor, Graham and the fleeing Gardeners were safely aboard, the weed that had choked the interior was dead, though not gone. Oozing brown vines still clogged the corridors. The clean-up began in earnest. It took several painstaking hours with gardening shears and secateurs, but at last the final remnants were removed and safely disposed of.

The Attendant was only too happy to lend a helping segmented foreleg in the clean-up. It had rendezvoused with the TARDIS shortly after they had left the doomed Gardener vessel, and it was not alone. Although one version of the Curatrix had unavoidably perished along with the warship when it flew into the sun, the AI was safely backed up in the systems of the Attendant's vessel.

They arrived on Tellus IV to deliver the Gardener refugees into the custody of Willow and her people. Graham's begonia was not among the survivors, but he had the oddest feeling that it was not the last time he would see the scheming houseplant.

With the TARDIS's console room back to its glowing best, the Doctor set the timeship in motion.

'One last stop,' she said.

Svalbard is a chain of islands that sits in the Arctic Ocean of planet earth, halfway between the Norwegian mainland and the North Pole. It is a remote and icy spot with few visitors. However, a recent group of tourists from the planet Sigma Deltiri had included it in their itinerary. The Deltiri come from a civilisation whose sole driving instinct is to visit a list of the greatest wonders in the universe. As soon as they are old enough to travel, they begin their journey, ticking off sites as they go, one generation after another, until they have seen everything. Which they never will.

Upon arriving in Svalbard, one Deltiran tourist pulled a sweater on over the T-shirt he had purchased in the gift shop on Shada, and commented to his brood-mate that the place was 'almost as cold as Calufrax Major'.

The tourists had come to see the famous Svalbard Global Seed Vault, which is located on the island of Spitsbergen. It is not open to tourists, but the Deltirans' interest lay not in the contents of the vault but in the interplay of the Arctic light with the building's remarkable exterior. Among beings like the Deltirans, who can see beyond the normal spectrum of human vision, the Global Seed Vault is regarded as a galactic wonder.

However, the Deltirans, like the rest of the galaxy, are unaware of its secret.

Along a hundred-metre tunnel and through a cold chamber lies the vault. Seeds from all over earth are safely stored here to protect ten thousand years of crop diversity from extinction by manmade or natural disaster.

But that is just the tip of a very deep iceberg.

The main chamber was empty when the TARDIS materialised. The handful of scientists who looked after the Global Seed Vault had returned to the nearby settlement of Longyearbyen for the night. Although, since it was summer, the midnight sun hung around like the hard-to-shift last guest at a party.

Inside the vault, the TARDIS dealt with the security cameras, so that its presence would go unnoticed. In the morning, when the scientists returned, they would find that, instead of logging the usual twelve hours of inactivity, their cameras had inexplicably recorded the yet-to-be-streamed new season of *Werelock Holmes*.

The Attendant marched down a narrow passage between shelves containing seeds from across earth. The Doctor and the others trooped behind the beetle.

'It seems that the First Gardener planned for just such a catastrophe,' it said. 'The co-ordinates appeared in my head the very moment that the Galactic Seed Vault was destroyed.' The Attendant stopped at the back wall, its mandibles clicking. 'The location of another vault. A backup.' It waved a foreleg across the wall's smooth surface, and the outline of a door appeared. 'It has existed as long as the other, and is just as big, with all the same seeds. But this one has a sauna.'

'Really?' said Ryan.

'No,' said the Attendant, pushing open the door.

Graham went to go through, but the Curatrix stepped in front of him, blocking his path. The holographic image's eyes blazed red. 'And where do you think you're going?'

'N-nowhere,' he stuttered.

'Your work is done. We thank you for your contribution to averting the end of all life in the universe.' The AI's words said 'gratitude', while its tone said 'back off'.

'D-don't mention it,' said Graham.

'I believe this is your responsibility now,' said the Doctor, passing Yaz's thermos flask to the Attendant. But as the beetle reached for it, a look of horror came over the Doctor's face and she snatched it away. 'Or it could be chicken soup.' Quickly, she unscrewed the cap, stole a look inside, resealed it and handed it over. 'No. Genesis Seed. All yours.'

They waited until the Attendant and Curatrix had passed through the entrance to the secret vault and the door had sealed itself up again, then made their way back to the TARDIS.

Ryan shook his head and muttered to himself.

'What's up with you?' asked Yaz.

'I still can't get over it. Key number two – Graham and I are almost eaten by a giant carnivorous mole. Key number three – you had it all along.'

'I know!' said the Doctor delightedly. 'How easy was that?'

'Not making it better, Doctor,' said Yaz, through gritted teeth. She gave Ryan a sheepish look. 'I did get stuck in a creepy corridor.'

Ryan sniffed. 'I hardly think that compares to what we went through. Do you?'

They went inside the TARDIS and gathered in the console room, as the Doctor began to hit switches with her usual enthusiasm. The controls hummed with power, the noughtweed already a distant memory.

'So, where to next?' asked Ryan.

The Doctor didn't seem to hear the question. She paused over one particular instrument panel, studying it intently. 'Hmm.'

'What is that?' asked Graham. 'Service indicator?'

'The distress-signal receiver. Clever piece of kit. Capable of tuning into signals sent from anywhere in the universe.'

The three companions clustered round, and Yaz motioned to a pulsing section of the display. 'I'm guessing the blinking light means someone's in distress?'

'Then what are we waiting for?' said Ryan.

'Whoa!' said Graham. 'What's the rush? "Distress" doesn't necessarily mean life or death, right? Come on, we've literally just saved the universe. Don't we get some time off?'

Ryan threw up his hands in frustration. 'Graham!'

'Don't "Graham" me. It could also be a trap. Right, Doc?'

'Could be,' agreed the Doctor brightly.

'That's not going to stop you rushing headlong in, though, is it?' added Graham miserably.

In answer, the Doctor shot him a grin.

'Ignore him, Doctor,' said Ryan. 'So, where to this time? Past, present or future?'

Yaz chimed in. 'Desert planet? Underwater city? Hogwarts?'

'That's just it,' said the Doctor, turning to stare with a mixture of puzzlement and unease across the console room. Slowly, she walked to the very edge of the room and gazed down the long passage that led to the deeper recesses of the ship. 'Based on the co-ordinates, the signal is coming from inside the TARDIS.'

ABOUT THE AUTHOR

David Solomons is the bestselling author of the *My Brother Is a Superhero* books, which have won the Waterstones Children's Book Prize 2016, the British Book Industry Awards Children's Book of the Year 2016 and the 2017 Laugh Out Loud Book Awards. He has been watching *Doctor Who* from behind a sofa since Jon Pertwee regenerated into Tom Baker. Writing *The Secret in Vault 13* fulfils a lifelong ambition.

In addition to his acclaimed children's fiction, he has been writing screenplays for many years – his first feature film was an adaptation of *Five Children and It*, starring Kenneth Branagh and Eddie Izzard. He was born in Glasgow and now lives in Dorset with his wife, the novelist Natasha Solomons, their son, Luke, and daughter, Lara.

ABOUT THE ILLUSTRATORS

Laura Ellen Anderson is the author and illustrator of the *Amelia Fang* series as well as the creator of *Evil Emperor Penguin* for The Phoenix comic. She illustrated Sibéal Pounder's *Witch Wars* series and CBeebies presenter Cerrie Burnell's picture books and fiction series. Laura's first author/illustrator picture book, *I Don't Want Curly Hair!*, was published in 2017. She has recently created new cover illustrations for Terry Pratchett's *Tiffany Aching* series, and Enid Blyton's *Famous Five* books. When not working, Laura enjoys doodling for fun, making 3D models of her characters, creating Harry Potter fan art, baking and making 'To Do' lists. She lives in North London.

www.lauraellenanderson.co.uk

@Lillustrator

George Ermos is an illustrator, maker and avid reader from England. He works digitally and enjoys indulging in (and illustrating) all things curious and mysterious.